(7)497-8337

3235
Satellite

building 400

Suite 105

Celeste O. Norfleet

Fast Forward

KIMANI
tru
™

Recycling programs
for this product may
not exist in your area.

FAST FORWARD

ISBN-13: 978-0-373-83134-0
ISBN-10:   0-373-83134-X

© 2009 by Celeste O. Norfleet

www.KimaniTRU.com

Printed in U.S.A.

Other Kimani TRU Books by Celeste O. Norfleet

Pushing Pause
She Said, She Said

To Fate & Fortune

Acknowledgments

To the young adults in my life who continue to show me that being young is just a state of mind. Also, a shout-out to all the readers who wrote telling me how much you enjoyed reading *Pushing Pause.* Your e-mails, letters and text messages were a joy to read. *Fast Forward* is for you—enjoy!

Please feel free to write me and let me know what you think. I always enjoy hearing from readers. Please send your comments to conorfleet@aol.com or Celeste O. Norfleet, P.O. Box 7346, Woodbridge, Virginia 22195-7346. Don't forget to check out my Web site at www.celesteonorfleet.com.

one

4 Real, I'm Fine

"All that other stuff is behind me now. I made sure of it. I don't even look back anymore. It's strange, like closing a door. But instead of being all nice about it, I slammed it, locked it, bolted it and then tossed the key. I'm done. It's time to fast forward."

—MySpace.com

I swear sometimes I think my life is a reality show and I just don't know it. The only things missing are commercial interruptions and that running thing at the bottom of the screen telling everybody about my mom, my dad and all my family drama. I can see it now, *Kenisha Lewis Exits the Fab Lane: The Way it Ain't, in Her Not So Real World*. The thing is, I keep waiting for the director to jump out and yell cut when my take's over. But it's not happening. 'Course everything else is.

See, my life was clicking along just fine until my dad dropped his bomb that dumped me and my mom at my grandmother's place in D.C. He was tripping as usual. His skank-of-the-month is a hoochie-momma reject with two—almost three—kids. They're supposed to be my sibs. I don't know. Whatever. Anyway, my mom died and I found out about my real sister. Things just went sideways after that.

I don't know exactly when it all started, but all of a sudden things are just fierce, and not in a good way. After the summer I went back to my old school, Hazelhurst Academy for Girls, thinking everything would be like it was before. But it's not. Nothing is the same. I guess 'cause I'm not the same. It's like I grew up overnight, and everyone else is just standing still. I keep wondering when it all changed. Was it when my mom died, or when I found out that my cousin is really my sister, or when my ex-best friend, Chili, got pregnant by my ex-boyfriend, LaVon?

It didn't take long for word to get around about my mom and dad. Everybody knew they broke up and that my mom died after that. It still doesn't seem real. I keep waiting for her to call me and tell me that I missed curfew. I still have her last message on my cell. I can't erase it. It just seems wrong.

Anyway, the only thing keeping me even halfway sane is hanging with my girls, Jalisa Saunders and Diamond Riggs. They're still the same. We still joke around, and we still go to Freeman Dance Studio. Yep, it's still our place. It's the freedom to kick it out that really keeps me going. After everything, I just go there and chill. All I have to do is get through this new drama.

So now I'm sitting here, waiting in front of the guidance

office. My turn is next. I know I'm gonna hear it, but it's not like I really care. I could say it wasn't my fault, but I know it was—at least some of it. I slapped her. But seriously, the shock on her face was worth it. She had the nerve to jump up in my face, so I handled it.

Open palm, all in the wrist, just like my mom said. 'Course, that started all kinds of screaming. Hazelhurst Academy girls don't fight, so the whole thing took less than three minutes to squash. But it was enough to get my point across. I guess she won't be up in my face next time. I smirked and looked across the open office space. Regan Payne was a skank with serious drama issues. We didn't like each other from way back in seventh grade. The only thing keeping me from whipping her ass back then was my grades. So now I'm done with all that. It doesn't matter anymore.

She's sitting across from me staring again like she think she wants to do something. You'd think she woulda learned by now. Her face was a mess. Well, I guess everything about her was a mess. She wore a hoodie to fight. That was so stupid. I grabbed hold and banged her face over half the lockers down the hallway. I'm not bragging. I really don't do the fighting thing, but I refuse to back down. So now she just keeps staring like she wants to go round two with me. "What?" I ask, in a threatening tone, "you think you want to step up in my face again?"

"Don't even think about it. Turn around." The gruff male voice made me look up seeing the security guard standing beside my chair. He had a bulldog face with a permanent frown that said he wasn't putting up with anything. Fine, 'cause for real this is so stupid. What did he expect me to do, jump up and start whipping on her again here in the main office? I think I made my point already. Her swollen bleeding lip and the weave tracks hanging out of her head was proof of that.

Anyway, a few minutes later my cell vibrates in my pocket. I already know who it is, either Diamond or Jalisa. They're my girls, even if they forget sometimes—forget to keep secrets—but we're still tight. They were there when it happened—when my mom died—by my side the whole time. You don't forget stuff like that. It was a long, hard summer, and by August things had just crashed and burned. I can't believe I actually thought September would be different, better. It wasn't.

I pulled out my cell and checked the number. I was wrong. It was LaVon. Seriously, I have no idea why that fool is still trying to talk to me. He knows his stupid behind is played out. I don't have time for his drama. And all that about him and Chili, he can keep that 'cause they sure 'nuff deserve each other.

"I know you don't intend to use that thing in here," the secretary said, eyeing me suspiciously, like I'd been holding a gun or something.

I looked at the cell phone in my hand then back up at her. She was always a pain in the butt. She acted like she owned half the school. "Get a life lady, you're a paper pusher, not queen of the world," I wanted to say that, but of course I didn't. "No, I was just checking the time," I said, as I closed the phone. "I don't have a watch anymore."

"It's third period, eleven forty-five," she snapped.

"Thank you," I said nicely and smiled hoping she actually thought I meant it. Man, going back to school was seriously harder than I thought. No lie, this place is working a sistah's nerves for real with everybody acting all strange and different. They should seriously check that stuff. The teachers were all sympathetic, and the students were just acting all stupid, more stupid than usual. Then it's the other side.

The jealous skanks that wanta step up in my face. Yeah, my candy-ass is still workin' it, after my mom, after my dad, after Chili and especially after LaVon. I'm still workin' it. That's why I had to step up and jump right back in Regan's face. She was getting all up on herself, like she don't know or something. I looked at her sitting there. She rolled her eyes. I just started laughing. This place is a trip. I don't know why I didn't see it before.

The door opened and Mrs. Hanover, the dean of students, stood waiting. She didn't say anything. She just stood there like I was supposed to be intimidated or something. Wrong. "Kenisha Lewis," the secretary said, rather than asked. Sitting behind her desk, she looked directly at me, I guess expecting me to flinch or something. Thing is, six months ago I would have. I would have just about peed my pants. Now, I just don't care.

"Yeah," I said standing, then sucked my teeth and rolled my eyes at Regan. It was childish, I know, but whatever. I was just so tired of all this fake drama. Everybody had something to say.

"Come in Kenisha," Mrs. Hanover said.

I walked over to the open door hearing the quiet chatter

of the silly student aides over by the copy machine. They were looking at me and whispering. For real, sometimes I really hate this place.

I walked into the office. My counselor, Mrs. Clarkson, was sitting talking to my dad. Five guesses who they were talking about. My dad watched as I sat down in the chair between him and Mrs. Clarkson. The disappointing grimace on his face didn't move me. If that's all he had, I was fine.

My dad's a trip like that. He plays this concerned father when he has to. But he's got so much going on that even I don't know how he handles it. He has a dead almost-wife, a wannabe wife who's pregnant and argues all night long. Plus I just know he's stepping out on her, mainly 'cause it's the same thing he did with my mom. The whole monogamy thing just isn't him. He's an old-time player still trying to work it.

"Kenisha, is there something you want to tell us before we get started?" Mrs. Clarkson said, trying to be as pleasant as possible. Believe it or not, I actually liked her before. She was kind and always gave you a platform to speak. But I wasn't in the mood to do the soft, tender thing. I guess I'm still too angry. So I looked at Mrs. Clarkson like she's nuts. Talk about a cliché. Is she for real? "No."

"If ever you want to talk, I'm here," she added, in that way she has that always makes you feel like you're five years old.

So I give her a blank stare. She is nuts. What does she want me to do—open up, cry, scream, say sorry? It ain't happening. It's like everybody expects me to be different. I'm not. I'm still the same as I was before. It's everybody else who changed.

Mrs. Hanover walked over and sat behind her desk. She turned to her computer and pressed a few keys. My transcript came up. "Kenisha, your father, Mrs. Clarkson and I have been discussing your problem…"

I stopped listening. First of all, I don't have a problem, they do. None of this would have happened if I didn't have to deal with all this stupid stuff.

"…counseling is a possibility…"

"…I have the numbers of some excellent child psychologists in the area…"

"I'm afraid we've gone beyond that…"

By the time school started three weeks ago my grandmother and father decided that it was best for me to continue going to Hazelhurst. My father suggested that I stay with him during the week then go to my grandmother's house in D.C. on the weekends.

"…your irrational outbursts will not be tolerated…"

"…given your exemplary scholastic past…"

"…we're of course deeply sorry for your loss…"

Whatever. They always talk around you but never to you. Everybody's sorry, everybody understands, everybody feels my pain. It's all crap. Nobody gets it but me. Mom died and left me alone to deal with all this. Dad has his pregnant girlfriend, my sister Jade has her man Ty, my grandmom has her church ladies and Terrence is in school.

"…we needn't decide today, but she needs help…"

"…my suggestion is to give her another chance…"

"…I think it would be best…"

"Kenisha, are you even listening to Mrs. Hanover?" my dad asked, knowing that I wasn't. "You need to pay attention. This is really important. This is your future."

"Yes," I hissed slowly.

"Perhaps after a semester or two Kenisha will feel ready to return. Of course at that time we'll be delighted to have her back with us. In the meantime we here at Hazelhurst are deeply saddened by your loss. Mrs. Lewis was a tremendous woman with exceptional skills. We will all miss her."

"Thank you. My wife was indeed a very special woman."

I half laughed, making a noise that sounded more like I was choking. I didn't intend to do it. It's just that he caught me off guard with that "my wife" crap. Newsflash James, Barbara was not your wife. She was the woman you lived with, had me with, then cheated on for a dozen or so years before she poured a medicine cabinet down her throat and died.

"Are you okay, dear?" Mrs. Clarkson asked.

I nodded, cleared my throat and covered my mouth. Mrs. Hanover got up and poured me a glass of water. She handed the glass to me then stood over me patting my back. It was strange, but I played along.

"The strain of my wife's loss has taken a burdensome toll on all of us. Most particularly Kenisha and myself," he added, reaching over and touching my hand. I was still holding my cell, so he took it and held my hand. "I don't know what I'm going to do with Barbara gone. She was everything to me. Her death was so tragic, so unnecessary. We're all just so devastated."

"Of course," Mrs. Clarkson said softly, "perhaps we can be a bit more understanding and patient."

Mrs. Hanover nodded, "Yes of course we understand, and we'll try to be more obliging given the uniquely tragic circumstances. But, Kenisha, you need to do your part as well."

"Do you hear that, Kenisha?" my dad asked.

I nodded. I had no idea how he did it, but my father had just wrapped Mrs. Hanover and Mrs. Clarkson around his finger and gotten me another chance. The man is seriously a player.

"Okay, Kenisha, this is it. Understood? We can't do this again. This is the fourth time you've been in this office in three weeks. Your past scholastic record is the only thing keeping you here right now. Do you understand? One more infraction of the rules and you will be expelled. I'll have no choice. That means you need to pick up your grades and start acting like you want to be here. You may go wait outside for your father."

I said thank you, then walked out leaving my dad in the office to do whatever damage control he intended to do. Of course the first person I saw was Regan standing talking with some of her girlfriends. They turned and stared at me as I walked over to the administrative assistant's desk to get a pass back to class. The security guard was there, too. I got my pass and was leaving the office with the guard behind me. Regan and her stupid girlfriends had nothing better to do than to call me a name on my way out.

The security guard heard them and jumped between us instantly. I was surprised. For a big man, he could really move. But it didn't matter. I wasn't going to do anything. I just got a reprieve. The security guard grabbed Regan and her two friends and pulled them into the dean's office. He mentioned something about them chiding and inciting trouble. I swear, I laughed all the way down the hall.

As soon as I got to the scene of the fight, Jalisa and Diamond were already standing at my locker waiting for me. "What happened?" they asked in unison, as if they'd practiced.

"They said you were in a fight," Jalisa said quickly.

"I was."

"Are you okay?" Diamond added. "What happened?"

"Yeah, I'm fine. Regan's not. She had the nerve to actually jump up in my face, so I smacked her. They called my dad and threatened to expel me, but then they gave me another chance," I said smiling, seeing the relief in both their eyes. Jalisa, Diamond and I have been best friends since we were four years old. Our moms took us to Freeman Dance Studio. We've been dancing and hanging ever since, except for a few months ago. But that's another story.

I opened my locker and grabbed my book bag. "My dad's still in the office talking to Mrs. Hanover and Mrs. Clarkson." I unzipped the outer pouch of my book bag and stuffed my chemistry lab book inside. I added my French textbook and my English literature book. They were all brand-new, never opened. Three weeks of school had already passed. I guess I should have done something by now, but I just wasn't in the mood.

"I hate the smell of a new book," I said, opening my

English lit book and flipping through the crisp, clean pages. The book made a loud crackling sound as the spine opened for the first time.

"You'd better get used to it. You got a lot of catching up to do," Diamond said.

"How the hell did you manage to get through the first three weeks of eleventh grade and not do a single homework assignment?" Jalisa asked, grabbing and opening my brand-new trigonometry book.

I took the book from her and tossed it back into the locker. "Just lucky I guess."

"Lucky my behind, you'd better step up," Diamond added.

"I still can't believe you have yet to turn in a chemistry assignment. Are you insane? Eleventh grade is serious college prep time," Jalisa added.

"Yeah, I know," I said, already tired of my girls giving me the whole "gotta do" drama.

"Seriously, Kenisha, we'll be applying to colleges this summer, and the grades we get now are the only ones they'll see first. That's why we have to up our game this year," Diamond said.

"Y'all can go ahead on and up your game," I told them.

"What about going to college?" Jalisa asked.

"Kenisha, don't you even care anymore?" Diamond added.

"Know what," I said turning to them, seeing them loaded down with textbooks, "truthfully, not at the moment. I'm just doing this to get through it." I seriously wanted to push the book bag and books back into my locker and just walk away. But I didn't. I just slammed it closed. I was getting tired of this conversation. Hell, I was getting tired of everything.

"Kenisha, girl, you need to chill out on that," Jalisa said. "You know how important college is. We've talked about colleges for months. Now all of a sudden, you're like, whatever. What's up with that?"

"Wait, Jalisa," Diamond said. "I know what she means. And I know exactly how she feels. We both do. Dealing with all this school stuff is crap compared to everything else. Remember how we felt?"

I went silent. We all knew what she meant. She was talking about my mom, and she was right. I looked at Diamond and then Jalisa. I knew they'd get it. When her grandfather died, Diamond was heartbroken. When Brian, Jalisa's older brother, started drugs and went all crazy, she was devastated. We were there for each other then. I guess I forgot that they'd be here for me now.

The first bell rang for fourth period. Each of our classes was on the other side of the building. That meant we had to hustle if we wanted to get there on time. I spun the combination lock and then slung my book bag on my shoulder.

"We'd better go," I said. Jalisa and Diamond nodded. "Since I got another chance, I'd better start off by being on time."

Then we started walking down the hall together.

"For real, I heard that. I have Mr. Cooper, he apparently trained with the friggin' Gestapo. The man has no clue as to the concept of chill," Jalisa said. We laughed as we approached the hall that would send us in three different directions. "Call me after class."

"Me, too," Diamond said.

"Crap—" it hit me "—my dad has my cell. I gotta get it before he leaves."

"We'll walk you," Diamond said. Jalisa nodded.

"No, don't be late to class. I have a note, remember?"

"Okay, see you later," Jalisa said.

"Call us," Diamond added.

"I will." I turned and hurried back to the main office. I was actually starting to feel a little better. Maybe I could get through this. Knowing that Jalisa and Diamond had my back was definitely making me feel better. I don't know what I was thinking. Of course they'd be there for me. They always are. So as soon as I opened the door to the main office, I saw that my dad was standing there talking to Mrs. Clarkson. "Dad, I need my cell back, and I gotta get to class."

"Actually, Kenisha, Mrs. Clarkson just sent a message to your fourth period teacher. You're excused the rest of the day."

Crap, what did I do now? This is the last thing I expected to hear. "I don't get it. I didn't do anything this time."

"Kenisha, we know you didn't do anything," Mrs. Clarkson said, using her silly, soft voice again. "Your father has some good news for you. It's going to help you tremendously. I'll let him tell you." She turned to my dad, smiled, offered her condolences again with a lingering-too long handshake and then told him that everything will get better. I was just standing there watching them wondering how soon he was going to add her to his harem. "See you tomorrow, Kenisha. Remember, you can always come to me anytime."

I nodded absently. My immediate concern was what the hell was going on now. "Come on, Kenisha. Let's go," my dad said walking away, expecting me to follow.

"Go where?" I asked without moving.

He turned smiling. "Mrs. Clarkson has generously asked a friend of hers to speak with you. He has some free time in about twenty minutes. We can just about get there on time."

"Wait, what, get where? I thought I was supposed to stay here and start getting my grades up."

"You are. You will tomorrow. Right now, you need to come on," he said. I slung my book bag on my shoulder, started walking, following my dad down the hall. "His name is Dr. Emmanuel Tubbs. I'm told that he's a nice guy. He's a psychoanalyst. He'll be—"

"A psychoanalyst, a shrink? What, you think I'm crazy now?" I asked, speaking louder than I intended. But it was just the shock that my dad had conspired to get rid of me, again.

"Kenisha, keep your voice down," he said quietly.

"You're trying to get rid of me again, just like before."

"Kenisha, calm down. Nobody's trying to get rid of you. Dr. Tubbs is a professional. I just want you to sit down and talk to him. There are things you apparently need to express, and I think this is good way for you to do it."

I was still in shock by the time we got to the car. My

dad was still spouting his propaganda about how much I need this, and how I'd feel so much better afterward. Isn't that the same thing they said about shock treatment? "Fine, whatever, I'm done."

two

Looking in the Mirror

"So I look in a mirror with a mirror behind me. I see myself over and over again. Maybe I've been wrong all this time. Maybe it wasn't me after all. Maybe all that other stuff happened to somebody else, maybe."
—MySpace.com

when you walk into a shrink's office and you see a couch you're expected to lay down and spill your guts. Uh-uh, I'm not having that. I plopped down in the massive chair and waited, so much for doing the predictable thing.

"Kenisha, why don't you tell me about yourself?"

"Didn't my father and Mrs. Clarkson already do that?"

"I'd like to hear from you, your words."

This was going to be a total waste of time. I rolled my eyes and looked around the room. It was a lot cheerier than I expected. I guess I assumed the place would look like what you see on television, all dark and gloomy. But the office was nice in a grown, no taste kind of way. So I continued looking around until I realized that Tubbs was actually sitting there waiting for me to say something about myself. "The model teenager, Kenisha Lewis is broken. Is that what you want to hear?"

"I'd like to hear whatever you'd like to tell me."

"I have a better idea. You tell me something. Why exactly am I here?" I asked.

"Your father is very concerned about you."

"Yeah, I bet."

"You're very angry. Let's talk about that."

Let's not. I was seriously not in the mood to have a deep philosophical discussion with a total stranger. So I sat in the shrink's office listening to him drone on about stuff he had absolutely no idea about. His name is Emmanuel Tubbs. What kind of name is that for a shrink? He's this old white guy, seventy- or eighty-something going on a hundred with absolutely no clue what my life was like as an African-American teenager in the twenty-first century. He didn't even have a computer or a laptop in the office. Please, what a joke.

So this was session one, a half hour in and I just nod and ignore him mostly. Maybe he'd shut up eventually. In the meantime I figure he's got a serious noisy, all-up-in-your-grill complex. I continued looking around checking out his crib.

He's got a million books on the shelves, and the office is bright. I seriously would have done a better job hooking him up. His has the typical college diplomas plus all these pictures of some man all over the walls, his lover maybe. Strange. He also has this half statue of I guess the same guy sitting, looking over his shoulder from the corner. Talk about an obsessive disorder. How am I supposed to take this man seriously when he has this weird guy everywhere staring at me? What a joke too. Talk about a Dr. Phil wannabe.

We played this word association game. He said a word and I had to say the first thing that came to my mind. Of course I deliberately messed with his head. He caught on after about the eighth time when he said umbrella and I said Uranus. I had to laugh. Afterward he got all serious on me and started asking how I feel about different things, like death. *Pleeease.* How do you think I feel, weirdo?

Psychoanalysts, I know what they are, mostly. At least I know what they're supposed to do. They're supposed to help a person deal with their emotional baggage by talking about past drama. Isn't that like everybody? Who doesn't have past drama?

"Kenisha, let's talk about your mother now."

I looked up at him. Okay, it was time to get this over with. I decided to change subjects to something more to my liking. "Is that your dad or your boyfriend?" I asked needing to make this last half-hour a bit more interesting at least.

"Excuse me," Tubbs said, I guess stunned that I actually spoke.

"Your boy there, his picture's on the wall?"

He turned. "No, that's Dr. Sigmund Freud. He was a brilliant and noted psychoanalyst. As a matter of fact, he's known as the father of psychoanalysis."

"So he's dead?"

"Yes."

"How does that make you feel?" I asked.

Tubbs smiled for the first time since he sat down. "We are not here to talk about my feelings, Kenisha."

"So what was up with him, anyway? I guess he was perfect, right."

"Far from it. It's widely speculated that he was addicted to cocaine even though he was a brilliant man with an enormous amount of courage and inner strength. It's also reported that he had oral cancer and suffered numerous surgeries."

"So that's supposed to excuse the fact that he was a druggie?"

"No, of course not."

"So why is it that when some guy like him is addicted, he's brilliant with inner strength. But when it's somebody on the street, a nobody, then they're a common criminal?"

"Excellent observation."

"It's not an observation. It's the truth," I pointed out.

"I completely agree. Society does have different standards according to who or what a person is. You're absolutely right, and I have no answer to your query."

I didn't expect him to agree with me. I thought he'd defend Freud and others, saying that they were special and deserved more consideration. "So what happened to him?"

"He committed suicide with the help of a friend."

"How'd he do it, bullet to the brain or by hanging himself?"

"Nothing so dramatic. He ingested lethal doses of morphine."

"Bummer."

"Indeed, but I prefer to be more inclined to his professional attributes such as his theories on repression, the unconscious psyche and the human defense method. I think maybe we should talk a little more about your defense methods."

"So the fact was that this guy was supposed to be all mentally brilliant and could dig deep into a person's psyche and everything. But at the end of the day he was actually nothing but a blow-head druggie? Doesn't that bother you? Not exactly a role model, ya think? I guess he should have just said no, huh?"

Tubbs, much to my amazement, started cracking up laughing. "You got me there, Kenisha. But let's get back to our previous conversation."

"I don't have anything to say," I said.

"If you don't talk to me, Kenisha, I can't help you."

"Finally you get it," I said. "See, you can't help me 'cause there's nothing wrong with me."

"No one is saying that anything is wrong with you."

"Liar, everybody's saying that."

He smiled and nodded then started writing something in his notebook. I figured all he was doing was a crossword puzzle or something like that. After a while he looked back at me. "Let's get back to your mother and your feelings. She died, I'm very sorry. Death can be hard, extremely hard, particularly an untimely death. Your father spoke to me briefly about her."

"Did he tell you his part in all this?"

"If you mean that he let her go from the house, then—"

"Let her go from the house? That's hysterical. Are you

kidding me? He kicked us out of the house so that he could bring his girlfriend in."

"Yes, I know."

"We had no place to go, and she blamed herself."

"Did you blame her also?" he asked.

The question surprised me. "No," I lied.

"Do you still blame her?"

"No," I lied again, "I don't still blame her for getting kicked out of the house. I'm fine with it."

"Do you blame her for leaving you, for dying?"

"No. What kind of question is that? How can I blame her for dying? Everybody dies. It was her turn." My voice cracked and I was starting to hurt again. I could feel the anger welling up inside. An explosion was coming. I needed to scream, to hit, to fight, but not to cry. No, not again, never again.

"It's okay to be angry, Kenisha. Your mother left you at a very—"

"Would you stop saying that she left me? She didn't leave me. She died. There's a difference. If she left me, there'd be the possibility that she'd come back. But she didn't leave me. She died. Get it? She's not coming back, ever."

"Let's talk about anger. Your anger."

"Let's not," I said, angrily.

"Anger is one of the seven stages of grief we all go through when death touches us. There's shock, denial, bargaining, guilt, anger, depression and finally acceptance. You're angry, Kenisha, understandably. But it's okay to be angry, angry at your friends, your family, your classmates, at yourself and most importantly, angry at her—your mother."

I looked up and glared at him. It took everything inside of me not to jump across the room, grab that stupid statue and beat him down. I dug my nails into my palms and prayed. That's what my grandmother always said to do when I feel angry. I prayed big time.

"Be mad at your mother, Kenisha. It's okay. Let it out, and let me help you get past it. Let's talk about—"

"No, let's talk about your mother," I snapped.

"My mother isn't the point of all this, Kenisha. We—"

"Humor me," I interrupted. He nodded and told me that his mother was fine and lived in Florida with his father, both retired doctors, blah, blah, blah. "See, you have zero experience with my drama. I'm a fifteen-year-old African-American girl, my mom's dead and my dad would rather I disappear. Bottom line, we have nothing in common."

"How do you feel about that?"

"About what?"

"About what you just said."

I looked at him like he was crazy. He must have seriously got it 'cause he looked down and started writing in his book.

"You got in a fight today. How do you feel about that?"

"I won," I said simply.

He scribbled in his notebook again. Then, as soon as he looked up to presumably ask me another silly question, a chime sounded. He grimaced looking annoyed. I presumed it was to end the session, so I got up and left. My dad was sitting out in the outer office waiting for me. He stood as soon as Tubbs and I came out of his office. "Well?"

"Well what?" I asked.

"What happened? Is she all right now?" he asked Tubbs.

I walked away. The implication that I was sent in for some kind of mental tune-up was so typical of my dad. He didn't do drama well. He caused it, spread it, passed it on, but never actually dealt with it.

Tubbs gave him some BS about me needing more sessions and contacting his secretary to set up a series of appointments. By this time I was too ready to leave. As expected, when we got in the car, the lecture started.

"Kenisha, I've done everything you wanted. You asked to go back to Hazelhurst. Fine, you're back. You asked to move back in during the week. Fine, the door's open, you're back." I didn't respond. So he continued a while longer, everything centered on how great he was and how good he'd been to me. Then he stopped and went quiet. "I know you blame me," he said softly, "I blame me, too."

"I don't blame you, Dad. I just don't get you."

"I miss her," he said.

"I miss her, too."

He pulled up in the driveway of his house—my old house. Leaving the engine running, he shifted to Park then turned to me. "You're gonna get through this, Kenisha. We both will. Here's your cell. I didn't want you distracted in the doctor's office."

I nodded, took my cell, grabbed my heavy book bag and got out the car. After I closed the door I looked back at him still sitting there with the engine running. "You not coming in?" I asked, stating the obvious seeing him shift the gear into Reverse.

He looked up at our used-to-be gorgeous house. "Nah,

I have things to do at the office. Tell Courtney I'll be home late."

I went inside. As usual, it hit me like a five ton anvil that things were different now. What used to be Bach, Beethoven, Brahms, Mozart and Rachmaninoff softly playing throughout the intercom sound system was now replaced with two yapping, screaming boys running around the house with two almost-dogs.

"Hi, loving family, I'm home," I said sarcastically, to no one. I plugged in my MP3 player and headed to my room. On the way, I stopped to deliver my dad's message to Courtney. It still felt weird to go to my mom's bedroom and see some other woman in there. Anyway, I dropped my earbuds and walked down the hall. I heard all this crying. I stopped at the half open door and listened.

Courtney was on the phone apparently talking to one of her skank girlfriends. The phone was on speaker, so I could hear both sides of the conversation. She was crying like crazy as the other woman tried to calm her down. *"Can you believe that asshole wants to name my baby girl Barbara, after that bitch?"* she said.

For calling my mom that I was seriously ready to walk in there and slap Courtney like before. But it was so damn ironic and funny. My dad wants to name Courtney's baby after my mom. What a trip.

"Now he's hanging out all the time. Every weekend it's the same thing. He says that he has all this work to do, but I know he's lying. I call the office or go by there. The place is all locked up. He's not even there. I know he's got

somebody else—probably that skank from his office,"
Courtney said.

"Don't worry about all that, girl. Whatever he's doing, leave him alone, chill and, seriously, stop nagging the man and checking up on him," skank girlfriend said.

"But what else am I supposed to do. Can you believe that I'm almost seven months pregnant with his third child, and he won't even touch me anymore? Not since she died. It's like he blames me or something. I didn't do anything. I told him to leave her, but he's the one who kicked her out of the house. I hate his ass. If I didn't have all these kids by him, I'd leave him."

"Then you should leave him," her friend prompted.

"And do what, go back to working at the gas station? No thanks. You know I think that the only reason he even comes home during the week at night is because of little Miss Shit. I swear, she's still walking around here like she owns the house. I can't stand her ass."

Okay, you know I'm cracking up smiling at this point. Serves her right, did she really think that my dad wasn't going to do the same exact thing to her that he did to my mom? Duh? So stupid.

"What am I supposed to do?" she asked, then started to cry again.

"I don't know, girl, but you need to step off the man's back. He's doing his best, ain't he? You there, right? But you should leave him," her friend said.

"He promised to marry me, now he's backing off on that. Talking about he doesn't want to upset Kenisha. Little Miss Shit, that's just bullshit. I'm so tired of his shit.

He needs to start treating me like I'm his woman and not some piece of ass he picked up someplace."

Through the receiver there was this real loud noise like a door slamming in the background and a man's voice was calling out. *"Listen girl, I gotta go,"* her skank girlfriend said quickly. There was a muffled noise like she was trying to cover the phone's mouthpiece or take it off loudspeaker.

"Who's that?" Courtney asked. *"What the…I know that's not…"*

Okay, my mouth dropped open, too. I swear I could have sworn I heard my dad's voice in the background telling girlfriend on the phone that he was home and wanted to get sexed up.

"Who the hell is that?" Courtney yelled.

"It ain't nobody you know, so stop trippn'. I told you I met this guy a while back, remember. Besides, your man is with little Miss Shit, isn't he?"

"Yeah, you right," Courtney said, calmer but still agitated. *"See, he got me trippin' on you now. So who is he?"*

"I'll talk to you later. I gotta go. See ya."

Courtney's friend hung up the phone. I heard Courtney blow her nose and was just about to go in and tell her what my dad said. "Bitch-heifer, I know that's my James over there," she muttered to herself.

Seeing Courtney was like seeing my mom all over again. She was sitting on the bed with her back to me. I glanced around quickly. The place was a mess. The bargain-basement cheap furniture looked like crap. Added to that, clothes were tossed and scattered everywhere. The bed was dirty and unmade and smelling like I have no idea.

"Courtney," I said quickly, happily, feeling better than I felt in a while.

She turned quickly, startled to see me. She actually jumped and looked at me, then the phone. I know she was wondering what I heard. So I just smiled like I do to drive her nuts. "What? Where's your dad?"

I shrugged. "He said he'd be late. He had some*one* to do."

"What?" she screamed.

"He said he had some*thing* to do," I said, changing the word *one* to thing.

She glared at me, her usual look, and hissed. "Don't you have something to do, other people to piss off?"

I just smiled and headed to my bedroom. I heard her crying all over again. Okay, yeah, a small part of me was feeling bad. Here the woman, almost seven months pregnant, not much older than me, was sitting crying because my dad was doing to her the same thing he did to my mom. But seriously, did she really expect he'd be faithful to her? Did she really think that she was the only one, even before all this happened?

three

Wait, I'm Not Done Yet

"I guess the more I learn about people, the less I really know. So when does the learning catch up with the knowing? When do people show who they really are?"
                                                                                —MySpace.com

I walked into my bedroom and closed and locked my door. I learned a while ago that those two boys of Courtney's like to barge into bedrooms. They did that to me once. I don't think it'll happen again. I dropped my book bag and plopped down on the bed. This is the only room in the house that had seriously nice furniture. Dad went all out spending all kinds of cash on my bedroom when I moved back in to go to school during the week. I know that pissed Courtney off.

When my mom left my dad, she took everything. I mean everything—even the doors off the hinges and the lightbulbs out of the sockets. When he brought Courtney here to live in my house, he had to start over from scratch. My mom put mostly everything in storage. Now that she's dead, I know where everything is—furniture, clothes, jewelry, computer files. Hell, I even know where the skeletons are. Of course Jade and my grandmother know, too.

My dad used to keep expecting me to return everything to the house, but I wouldn't. He thought that the storage place was going to call wanting payment. What he doesn't know is that my mom paid for two years. After that it'll still be tight. 'Cause my mom's insurance policy is seriously plump. She put away a ton of cash for me and Jade and grandmom.

As soon as I lie back on my bed my cell rings. I looked at the caller ID. It was LaVon, so I closed my eyes, ignored him and let it ring. When it stopped I opened my eyes and looked up at the ceiling. There was this little piece of tape still stuck up there from when I was twelve or thirteen years old. I taped a picture of Nelly on the ceiling so that I would see him as soon as I woke up every morning.

I had a serious crush. Thank God that was over. I stared at the tape while my mind wandered. It was something about what Mrs. Hanover said that made me start thinking. She said that I needed to start acting like I wanted to be there. That's just it. I wasn't sure I did, but I didn't know anyplace else to be.

My cell rang again. It was LaVon, again. I answered. "What?"

"Hey, Shorty, I was just thinking about you, what' up?"

"What do you want LaVon?" I asked dryly. I swear he never called me so much when we were actually supposed to be together as a couple. I always called him, and he always said that he was just about to call me, but he never did.

"Is that how it is? You acting all mean still. Girl, you know you need to chill with all that. I said I was sorry. Chili is lying. That ain't my kid. I swear."

"LaVon, it really doesn't matter 'cause I don't really care. Doesn't that tell you something?" He didn't answer. I guess he was trying to think. My patience for his stupid stuff was seriously burnt out. "I gotta go, you need to call Chili and start buying some baby clothes."

"See, it ain't even about all that. I told you she lying."

"Whatever, I gotta go. Bye." I closed my cell. His whole drama is too pathetic. I wondered what his boys would say about his sorry butt now.

I lay back and closed my eyes. I know I wasn't going to sleep because I wasn't really tired. I just lay there with my eyes closed listening to myself breathing, waiting. I was thinking about my day. It was strange. I started thinking about the fight and how I just went off on Regan. Yeah, we didn't get along and she called me a name but, hell, I called her so many names in the past I need to check and make sure I know her real name. So, I wondered why I went off on her like that. I guess I was mad, and she was in the wrong place at the wrong time.

I was thinking about being mad when my cell rang. It was Jalisa and Diamond. We talked for a while then I told them that LaVon was trying to step up again. We laughed about that for awhile. Jalisa told us that she saw Chili hanging around school. She didn't speak. No big surprise there. We were trying to figure out why she was all pissed off at us when we should be the ones pissed off at her.

After all, she out and out lied to my face, snuck around

behind my back with LaVon and tried to blame everything on Diamond. If anyone should be upset, it should be me. But I wasn't really—not about that drama anyway.

"So where did you go after school? We stopped by your locker and you never showed up," Diamond said.

"You will not believe this. Mrs. Clarkson and my dad put their heads together and got me an appointment with a shrink. I left school early and had a session with him."

"What did he say?" Jalisa asked.

"How did it go?" Diamond added.

"I wasn't about to be talking to some old guy. Besides, there's nothing wrong with me."

"Except that you're always mad," Jalisa said.

"I am not," I insisted.

"Yes you are, Kenisha, and you know it. But we understand. I was pissed when my grandfather died," Diamond said.

"And I'm still pissed about Brian. Why in the world would he start smoking crack? I swear I still don't get it. Now we have no idea where he is or what he's doing. My sister, Natalie, said that she thought she saw him about a month ago in D.C."

"For real?" Diamond asked.

"Yeah, but she wasn't sure. I just don't get it, and yeah, I'm still pissed at him."

"Yeah, but I'm not pissed. I'm fine."

"Kenisha," Diamond said.

"Come on girl, denial much, you know you mad," Jalisa added.

"I am not mad," I said firmly.

"Fine, whatever, it looked mad to me," Jalisa said.

"I'm not mad," I repeated.

"I'm not talking about you," Jalisa said. "I'm talking all those weave tracks in the hall and in the trashcan at school."

"Ohhh, that was too much. Did y'all see that trash can? It was filled with fake hair. You know Regan's mad now," Diamond said laughing. We all broke up laughing by this time.

Regan wasn't exactly Miss Congeniality at school. That's why nobody really liked her except her clique. She thinks she's cute and she slings that weaved-in hair around all over the place, acting like it's hers. Everyone knew it wasn't. One time somebody actually cut some off in the back. She had the weird square thing going on in the back of her head. She didn't know about it until her girls told her. She was too pissed. The next day she said that it grew back overnight. Oh, please.

So we laughed about that some more then talked about homework assignments. Since none of us had classes together, we just talked in general about the classes and assignments. After a while we decided to get some homework done. I had a lot of catching up to do. Diamond and Jalisa offered to stop by and help, but I told them that I could do it. So we hung up, and I got busy.

Three hours later I had gone through my chemistry, English, U.S. history and French assignments. I had so much work to catch up on. I just started at the end and worked my way back. I opened my trigonometry book and started flipping through the pages. Since I'd only been half paying attention in class I seriously needed help with the assignments so I wrote myself a reminder to stay after school tomorrow. Next I grabbed the book for English lit class. It was *Lysistrata*. It was written in 411 B.C. I got halfway through the first page and fell asleep.

I woke up an hour later. My cell was buzzing. It was Jalisa. "Hey."

"We're on our way over. Meet us outside."

It was early and I had gotten a lot of homework done, so I decided that I deserved a break. We went to the mall. Diamond drove. We walked around a little, but since none of us was sporting the kind of cash we used to have over the summer, we just hung out at the food court.

"So you gonna see the shrink again?" Diamond asked out of the blue. I shrugged. "I think you should." I looked at her like she was nuts. "Seriously, sometimes you just need to talk."

"I thought that's why I had y'all as my girls," I said.

"Yeah, you got us," Diamond said.

"But we're biased. We your girls. What the hell do we know?" Jalisa added.

I could tell they had already talked about this. But I wasn't in the mood to get all dramatic about it, so I just changed the subject. "I heard Gayle Harmon's coming back to Freeman. She might be teaching a class."

"Seriously, for real? Who told you that?" Diamond said.

"No wait, for real? Jade told you, right?" Jalisa added.

I laughed. Seeing Jalisa and Diamond's eyes all wide and bright was funny. They were seriously starstruck ever since I told them that my sister Jade and Gayle had me dancing with them making up steps for Tyrece's new video. Although it was on the down low for everybody else, they knew that Jade and Tyrece were engaged—and that I had the 411 when it came to information.

"Nope, Jerome told me," I said.

"Jerome? Jerome who? We don't know no Jerome," Jalisa said.

"Yes, we do. Jerome Tyler."

"You mean, Li'l T?" Diamond asked. I nodded.

"Are you kidding me," Jalisa said. "You got me all excited over something Li'l T said. Girl, please, you know that boy can't get anything right. He's a kid. What is he, six?"

I laughed. Li'l T was small for his age, and people were always getting on him about something he thought he heard. He had a way of hearing sensitive information that nobody else knew. "No, seriously, that's what he told me. I was at my grandmother's house last weekend, and he told me that he overheard Ms. Jay in her office talking about it."

"Maybe he got it right this time," Diamond said.

"Please, Li'l T getting something right? He doesn't have a clue," Jalisa insisted. "Y'all listening to that fool. He probably heard Ms. Jay ordering a pepperoni pizza." We broke up laughing. Jalisa always did that to us. She would say outrageous stuff and get us laughing.

After that we started talking about everything: dance class, when we were in elementary school, parties, guys, movies, clothes, school. The conversations shifted so fast that anyone listening might have thought we were crazy. Then these four guys came and sat at the table next to us. They checked us out and we looked at them, but that was as far as it was going. We all knew it. So we did what we usually did to shoo flies away.

The three of us had been taking French since grade school. We were good, real good. So when we kinda suspected that someone was listening in on our conversation, we started speaking French. It usually threw people off. The four guys sat a while trying to figure out what was going on, and then they eventually walked away. We burst out laughing, of course.

"Come on. I gotta get my mom's car back," Diamond said.

We started walking back through the mall. On our way out we saw LaVon and some of his friends. Without saying a word, we took a serious detour before he saw us. The last thing I needed was his drama. So we were walking through the parking lot, and we saw Chili's car. Jalisa and Diamond looked at me. "I don't even want to hear it."

"You know she coming back to school for good, don't you?"

"When?" I asked.

"I thought she got transferred," Jalisa said.

"I heard she was coming back Monday."

I didn't say anything. First almost running into LaVon and then finding out that Chili would be back in school. That was enough for me. Diamond and Jalisa changed the subject, thankfully. They started talking about getting together and helping me with some of my class assignments. None of us had classes together, but we did have some of the same teachers. We made a plan to crash over at Jalisa's house the following night. It would be Friday, so it was perfect. After that I could keep right to my grandmother's house in D.C.

By the time I got to my dad's house, I was tired—but in a good way. We laughed too much and ate too much at the mall. We had a cheeseburger, a hot dog, loaded cheese fries, a salad and a cookie. Everything was always split into thirds. Hanging out with Diamond and Jalisa always made me feel better no matter what drama I was dealing with. I couldn't imagine not hanging with them. We were best friends forever. We knew each other's pain and joy, and none of that mattered. We always promised that we'd be best friends through thick and thin, no matter what.

I walked in the house and heard talking in the dining room. I figured everybody was eating dinner. I wasn't hungry so I decided to keep up to my bedroom and do some more studying. Plus, I was determined to figure trig out. I got halfway up the stairs when I heard my name.

"Kenisha," my dad called out.

I sighed heavily, came back downstairs and went into the dining room. "Yes?"

"Can't you speak when you come in the house?"

"Sorry, I didn't want to disturb. Hi, Dad, Courtney, Banana-head, Coconut-head." I had nicknames for the boys that changed daily. The boys laughed and began arguing who was which name.

"Jr., Jason, eat your food," Courtney snapped sharply.

"Where were you?" my dad asked.

"I went to the mall with Jalisa and Diamond."

"I thought you had homework to do," he continued.

"I did homework all afternoon. All I need to do now is study. That's what I was gonna do when you called me in here."

"Are you hungry? Courtney fixed spaghetti for dinner."

I looked at the red mush sitting in the plastic Tupperware bowl. It looked like brain surgery gone bad. I tried not to look disgusted, but, for real, the stuff made me feel nauseated. "No thanks, we ate at the mall." Yuck, I swear I may never eat anything red again.

"Why don't you get a plate and join us," he said.

"Nah, I'm okay, for real," I said.

"Well, have a seat. I want to talk to you."

I sat down and noticed that Courtney never even looked up at me. She was in her mad mood as usual. "Courtney, why don't you get Kenisha a plate and a fork?"

"She said she's not hungry, James," she hissed.

"I gotta study." I said standing and taking a step back. There was no way I was eating that stuff. I looked at the bowl again, then at the boys. They were watching me and making the same face I did. I chuckled seeing them.

To tell the truth they weren't all that bad. They made me laugh, mostly when they were driving Courtney crazy, which was all the time. She was forever yelling and threatening them. At times I actually made it worse by provoking them like now. I made another face at the bowl of mashed brains.

"I don't wanna eat this no more. It looks nasty," Jr. said.

"Me, too. No more. It's nasty," Jason said.

"Y'all eat y'all food now," Courtney snapped.

They looked at me. I winked, and they broke up laughing. Courtney snapped her head up at me. I smiled nicely, and she rolled her eyes. The thing was, the boys listened to me more than they listened to her, and that always pissed her off.

"So are you ready to tell me what you talked to Tubbs about?"

"Freud mostly," I said.

"Who's Tubbs?" Courtney asked.

"Kenisha's counselor at school set up an appointment for her to talk to a friend of hers. He's a psychoanalyst."

"Wait, we're paying for her to see a shrink now?"

"I'm paying for my daughter to speak with a doctor," James said pointedly.

"Same thing. First she gotta go to that expensive private Hazelhurst Academy for Girls that cost a damn arm and a leg, then she takes dance classes in D.C. and now she gets to see a shrink. How much is that costing us?"

"It doesn't matter how much it's costing me, Courtney."

"Hell, yeah it matters. What if I want the boys to take dance lessons or soccer or swimming lessons?"

"Then they will—later—when they're ready."

"See, that's just wrong," she complained raising her voice. "What you need to do is send her back down to D.C. with her grandmother so that we can get back to our lives. I'm tired of this half stepping you doing around here. She gets everything she wants, and now she got the boys not eating."

"How did I get the boys not to eat?" I asked.

"You did something," she accused. I looked at the boys and winked. They broke up laughing again.

"See? See what I mean?"

"Kenisha stop it. Courtney, chill," Dad said. "She winked and made them laugh. What's the big deal? They're her brothers. They're getting along. What's wrong with that?"

"You never see things my way anymore," she complained.

I winked again. The boys laughed and fell off the chairs. My dad and Courtney looked at me. "Sorry. Starburst, Skittles, sit upright and eat your stuff," I said, exerting my control of the boys. They immediately sat back in the chairs and started eating again.

"See, she got them to eat. That's good, right?" Dad said.

I tried so hard not to laugh. Courtney looked like she was ready to blow steam out of her ears. This was so much better than the first time I walked in and saw her playing queen of the manor in my mom's house. I slapped her then, but I found a better way to piss her off. I was being nice.

Courtney was pissed, but it had nothing to do with me or Tubbs or the boys not eating. She was mad 'cause she knew that more than likely my dad was stepping out on her with her girlfriend. My mom had been there, done that. So the argument started. She was yelling about money and how much she didn't have, my dad was going on about how he gave her enough and my two half brothers were tossing spaghetti mush at each other. As usual I just watched the drama until I'd had enough, then went to my bedroom. Seriously, that was the best spaghetti dinner I never had.

four

No Big Surprise

"When you make four right-hand turns, you wind up in the same spot you were in when you started. Okay, now what? I've been running so far and so much, faster and faster, that I found myself running in circles."

—MySpace.com

of course nothing ever turns out like we expect. After I left the hot and heavy argument between Courtney and my dad, then Courtney and the kids, then Courtney and my dad again, I studied then crashed. I dreamt about my mom and woke up almost late for school. I was in such a rush that I forgot to grab my trig book. *Crap*. I guess staying after wasn't gonna happen.

So first thing in the morning I'm sitting there with just my notebook without a clue. I'm usually really good at math, and algebra wasn't bad at all. I actually understood it. Then I passed calculus with a B+ last year, but trig and the study of triangles was kicking my butt. Maybe I just wasn't seeing it right. Sine, cosine, tangent, perpendicular, hypotenuse, adjacent. Get real, it's a triangle. At least calculus had speed and motion. Whatever. Ninety minutes later, I breezed through U.S. history. No big deal.

Friday morning English lit class, I was sitting there trying to act like I read the assigned chapters of *Lysistrata*. But having surfed and checked out Wikipedia, Spark-Notes, CliffsNotes and talking about it with Diamond and Jalisa, I got the general idea of the book. So I'm sitting there listening to the discussion and even answering a few questions when Chili walks in. I swear, everybody turned around to look at me. I ignored all the drama and just waited for class to be over.

When the bell rang, I was the second one out the door. I dumped my history book in my locker, rolled my eyes at Regan and her girls then headed to lunch. I found Diamond on the way, and Jalisa was already in line getting her food. We sat together. I told them about trig, and they said they'd help so that was tight. After lunch, we sat outside chilling.

"So what are you gonna do for your sixteenth birthday Sunday?" Diamond asked. I shrugged. I didn't exactly forget about it. I just pushed it aside for the time being. "We can hang out," she offered.

"Why don't we hang out at my house? I'll get my mom to grill, and we can just sit out and chill—maybe check out a movie afterward."

"I don't know. My dad might be doing something. I'll let you know." Actually I had no idea what I was going to do, or if my dad was even planning something. He didn't say, and I didn't ask. Since I'd be over at my grandmother's house, I assumed he'd stop by there. At any rate, I didn't want to talk about it.

But before I could change the subject, we looked up as Chili Rodriguez walked by. We couldn't help but see her baby bump. Yep, she was definitely showing now. Nobody said a word. Of course she wasn't the first to get pregnant at sixteen, but I guess it was different when you actually know the person. I just looked at her. I couldn't even imagine what she was about now. We hadn't actually talked since the day I heard her leave a message on LaVon's answering machine about him stepping up and taking care of his responsibilities.

Man, that was some serious drama, but I handled it. Truth was, I was about done with him anyway. His drama had played out. All he wanted was to get with me, and I wasn't ready for all that. When I called him on his crap, he swore that Chili went after him and that the baby wasn't his. She wanted him to step up 'cause of his NBA prospects. It was like a daytime soap opera up in there. But I wasn't about to be in their continuing saga. I left that alone quick.

Later, I heard that both their parents were involved. Everybody was tossing accusations around. They had lawyers and doctors and even a DNA specialist. Crazy stuff. I'm just glad he and I never got together like that. Ruining my life over a minute of ohh-ahh is definitely not worth it. Beside, didn't they ever hear about STDs? No way, hell, no, I'm waiting, period.

So Chili walked by and eyed us, but we didn't even go there. We just started talking about English lit class and *Ly-*

sistrata. We were laughing about how the Greek men must have been shocked to come home to the ultimatum. Then the conversation shifted a few more times. When we started talking about going to Freeman for dance class Saturday morning, the bell rang. We split up and headed to class.

French class was next for me. I knew it would be a breeze. Since the day was just about over, I figured all I had to do was chill and coast into the weekend. I was standing at my locker getting my stuff and looking for the French assignment I knew I completed last night when I heard Chili talking behind me. I ignored her. She just wasn't worth it.

"What did you tell LaVon about me?" she asked again.

Yeah, I knew the voice. Nobody had that baby voice like Chili. It was nerve-racking, slow with an almost lisp because she pouted her lips when she talked. She thought the guys liked it. Maybe they did. I always thought she sounded like Minnie Mouse on crack. But that's just me.

"I know you hear me talking to you, Kenisha. What did you tell LaVon about me?"

"Chili, you and I have nothing to talk about," I said, continuing to go through my locker looking for my French assignment.

"He told me that y'all getting back together again," she said.

I rolled my eyes. I seriously didn't need this drama, so I just kept doing what I was doing. I could tell that other students were stopping and waiting, expecting me to do something. But they'd have a hell of a wait 'cause I was going to just ignore her.

"You always want what I got, always going after my

leftovers. That's why nobody like you now. You knew me and LaVon was tight. That's why you jumped on him from the start. He wanted me, but you stepped up in his face. So what are you gonna do now?"

I started laughing. She was talking fast, and I doubted anybody could even understand her. When she got excited or nervous, she'd talk a mile a minute. But, whatever, I had no intention of playing her game. The first warning bell rang, and I found my French assignment in my U.S. history notebook. I grabbed it, stuffed it in my class book and slammed my locker.

"Don't be laughing at me, skank. This shit ain't funny."

I turned around and stared her up and down. She was just too pathetic. And I swear I couldn't believe what she was wearing. Hazelhurst Academy for Girls had a strict dress code, but she was stepping out with her skirt hemmed up to her butt and a white shirt too tight and two sizes too small that made her fat boobs stick out like a couple of honeydew melons.

"Your stupid girls ain't here with you now, so you ain't got nothing to say. Yeah, look, heifer, that's right. I'm pregnant with LaVon's baby, and he gonna take care of me all the way to the NBA. When he signs that contract, I'm gonna be right there with him."

"Look Chili, you want LaVon. I told you before, he's all yours. Talk about leftovers. Take him, 'cause I sure don't want him. And as for him signing that NBA contract right out of high school, I'd check that box later if I were you. He's not getting anything. So the best you'd better hope for is to watch him playing basketball on the corner."

"You just mad 'cause I slept with him and you didn't."

"Yeah, like I'm really mad about that," I said sarcastically. A few of the girls standing around started laughing at that remark. "See, I still got my whole life ahead of me. No drama, no diapers, no baby and no LaVon. I think I got the better deal out of all this," I said, then turned and walked away.

"You are such a skank, Kenisha. That's why your papi dumped your ass and you moms killed herself," she snapped nastily. I felt my body stiffen but I just kept walking. I knew she was just trying to provoke me. But I wasn't having it. I could hear the other girls really talking now. Everybody knew that my mother died over the summer, but it wasn't out there exactly how it happened. "Yeah, that's right chica. Your moms killed herself to get away from your ass."

I heard the security guard call out from down the hall. I kept walking, and a lot of the onlookers scattered and hurried to class. I figured all I had to do was get to class. I'd be late, but at least I wouldn't have to deal with her crap. She was not going to get the best of me. I was stronger than that. My mom made me stronger than that. Just then I felt a push on my back. I stumbled forward then turned around and glared at her. I glanced over her shoulder seeing the security guard running toward us. I did not need this.

Chili had the nerve to be standing there with her hands on her hips looking at me. "Yeah, I pushed you, skank. What you gonna do about it? What you gonna do, Kenisha?"

I turned and kept walking. I was not going to ruin my

chance here because of her drama. I got to my French class and opened the door to enter. Just as I did, she pushed me again. I stumbled and dropped my books. Everybody in the class looked up. "You just like your moms, a scared-ass bitch who can't hold on to a man. Why don't you go do what she did?"

It might have been wrong to whip on a pregnant girl, but she went too far and I went off. No, I didn't need a hoodie to tear her ass up. We were both pissed, so we were getting as good as we were giving. My French teacher intervened, and the guard showed up. The fight broke up almost instantly. Ten minutes later, I was sitting in the dean's office with the security guard standing next to me. Chili sat across the room nursing her lips and crying about her baby and how I tried to kill her.

Please. I heard her, but all I was thinking was how I could fast-forward this drama and get it over with. Forty-five minutes after that, I was cleaning out my locker when my girls, Diamond and Jalisa, showed up. They stood on either side, eyes wide open in shock. "They kicked you out, didn't they," Diamond asked. I nodded.

"Damn, ain't that some crap," Jalisa added.

"So what happened?" Diamond asked. "What did they say?"

"I got expelled."

"You mean detention, like before, right?" Jalisa said.

"Nope, I'm expelled. I'm supposed to clean out my locker and report back to the office. I'm out of here as of today."

"Wait, they expelled you for what, fighting Chili? I heard she provoked it."

"That's right. That means it wasn't even your fault. I heard that the security guard said Chili provoked it, too. Seriously, Chili is a skank with drama. Everybody knows that."

"I knew we should have all walked to class together," Diamond said.

"Yeah, we could have jumped her ass," Jalisa hissed.

"Nah, you guys need to stay out of this mess," I said.

"What if we tell them that we saw her hit you first," Diamond whispered as she moved closer.

"Yeah, and that you were only defending yourself," Jalisa added moving closer, too. "They'll believe me, I'm class president, and Diamond has been on the honor roll since kindergarten."

"Nah, y'all can't be getting in trouble like that. I'm fine, for real. Besides, the guard already said that. He saw her push me twice. But then he also saw me punch her in the face. You know, I'm just tired of all this drama here anyway."

We stopped talking and turned around. Chili walked by smirking at us. She was red and bruised, and her lower lip was puffy and split.

"I should beat her down some more, but the last thing I want is for everybody to think I was doing it because of LaVon. I wasn't."

"Girl, we know that."

"Don't nobody think that. Everybody know she's just a wannabe poser."

"She's just jealous—always was, always will be," Diamond said.

"But seriously, I've never seen her look better. Her split lip and bruised face looks so much better that all than makeup she usually wear," Jalisa joked. Both Diamond and I burst out laughing. All this drama coming down on me and I'm standing in the hall with my girls laughing my head off.

"Seriously, LaVon dumped her butt anyway. I heard he's gonna get a DNA test 'cause that ain't even his baby," Jalisa said. "That's probably why she's so pissed at you."

"Whatever, I'm not stressing over that. They deserve each other. I just don't want it said that I was fighting her 'cause of him."

"You still going to Freeman tomorrow?"

"I doubt it," I said thinking about all the times I couldn't wait to get to Freeman and dance. That was my thing. I loved to dance and I was good, seriously good. Hell, I even danced with Gayle Harmon. But that seemed like a long time ago. But, for real, it was only last month. A lot happened in a month.

Jalisa and Diamond helped me take the stuff out of my locker. Then we took the long way back to the main office. School was over for the day, so there was hardly anybody in the halls, but still, no sense rushing. Hazelhurst Academy for Girls was where I spent my life since kindergarten. Now it had turned its back on me just like everything and everyone else.

five

Commercial Interruption

"It's not like I didn't know it was coming, so I wasn't all that pressed when it happened. Freedom is something you desire but never get. It's intangible, illusive and always just a step away from my reality. Hey, anybody seen my freedom?"

—MySpace.com

I swear if I could scramble my DNA I would. I'd change who I was, where I was and how I was. Instead, I sat at the dining room table listening to my dad go off on me all night. Courtney, sitting there smiling, was loving it, of course. All she kept saying was I told you so. And my dad was all over that.

"I gave you everything, and this is what you do in return? I told you not to get into more trouble. The school warned you no more trouble and what do you do the very next day, you get into a fight. Now the only way to get back in is to take the admissions exam in October. What is wrong with you?"

"Nothing is wrong with me," I said in my defense.

"I don't know what the hell we're gonna do now. You can't go back this semester. That means you need to get yourself enrolled someplace else until the new year."

"It wasn't my fault," I said, still pissed that I had to pick up the pieces of my life because of Chili's stupid drama.

"I'm through with this, Kenisha. That excuse is running thin with me. Nothing is ever your fault. You fought a pregnant girl. What's wrong with you?"

"Did it ever occur to you that she started it, and I was just defending myself? The security guard was right there. He saw her push me twice."

"Which apparently is the only thing stopping them from expelling you permanently. You should have walked away."

"See, I told you James. She's nothing but a trouble-maker. When she slapped me last month, you should have kicked her ass back then. She has no respect for anybody. I say kick her out."

"You don't have to kick me out," I said standing, "so don't bother, I'm already out." I turned and walked away.

"Kenisha, get back here. We're not through yet. You got expelled. That means we need to get you in someplace else."

"I say send her ass to public school," Courtney demanded.

"My daughter isn't going to public school. We'll get a tutor for a few months. Barbara would want that."

"Why the hell not public school? I went to public school, and ain't nothing wrong with me. I turned out fine," she said proudly.

"I didn't say anything was wrong with public school

Courtney, I went to public school, too—and so did Barbara."

"Do you have to mention her name every five seconds? I'm so sick of hearing about her I don't know what to do."

"Look Courtney, Hazelhurst Academy is where Barbara wanted Kenisha to go, and that's where she's going back. I'm not enrolling her in public school just to pull her out again. A tutor for the next few months will be fine."

"Hell, no. How much is that gonna cost?"

"Don't worry about the money," he said.

"Well, have her ass pay for it then. I know she got that fat insurance policy. She's sitting on all that money from her mother, and we got to fork over cash to get her a tutor. No, uh-uh. That's wrong."

"Whatever money Barbara left Kenisha and Jade belongs to them. I'm Kenisha's father. I'm paying for the tutor. Barbara would have wanted it."

"There you go again. Barbara this, Barbara that." My dad gave Courtney that look, and she went off on him. "What, you trying to say something, James? Do I embarrass you? Is that why you don't take me out anymore? Are you sick of hearing me complain? Well, I'm sick of hearing about her."

"This isn't about you, Courtney."

"Yeah, it is. You think I'm not good enough for you. Why? 'Cause my name isn't Barbara? Well, I am..."

Okay, as usual Courtney turned everything around to be about her. She lit into my dad and forgot all about me. I'm not saying that I was upset, but at the moment I had other things to deal with, and sitting here listening to her rage on at my dad wasn't working.

"…I am so sick of you acting like I'm nothing and she's all that. If Barbara was so damn good then why did you come after me…"

I was watching my dad and seeing him just sitting there. He wasn't even trying to argue back. By now Courtney was all up in his face screaming. She went on and on about my mom and how my dad used to complain about her. I sat listening, hoping she didn't know what she was talking about, but I kinda knew she did. I knew my dad had complained about my mom. So what Courtney was saying wasn't all that surprising. It sounded just like something my dad would say. 'Cause it was what I used to say.

I'm thinking about doing that fast-forward thing again. Pushing a button and getting this drama over with. I seriously wish I could do that right about now.

They went on for a while longer until my dad got tired and ended it. He sent me to my room, but I still heard Courtney muttering as she stomped around the house. My dad went out, and the boys were already doing a sleepover with friends. Nobody was in the house except me and Courtney. I lay across my bed and closed my eyes ready for whatever came next. Nothing did. I didn't intend to fall asleep, but I guess I did 'cause I woke up and it was light outside.

Saturday morning. I got up early and started dumping my stuff into my suitcase. I left my school uniforms in the closct but took the rest of my clothes and everything else.

I hated the idea of running away. It felt like I was being my mom all over again. I remember the last time I packed to leave this house. I was so upset, but that was before I knew what was really going on.

This time it's my choice. I thought I could do this, but I can't. Being here reminds me too much of before when my mom was alive, so I'm going back to my grandmother's house. I also decided what I'm going to do about school. I'll ask my grandmother to enroll me in Penn Hall High. It's right around the corner from her house, so getting there would be no problem. I'll go first thing Monday morning. But right now I needed to get to D.C.

I called a cab then started carrying my things downstairs. "Where do you think you're going?" Courtney asked, seeing me bringing my things down.

"Where you going, Kemesh?" Jason asked, standing looking up at me still in his Power Rangers pajamas. "Can I go, too?"

"No dummy, she's going to school," Jr. said.

"Nah-uh, cartoons is on. Can I go, too?"

"Not this time, little man," I said looking out the side window for the cab.

"I asked you a question, Kenisha. Where do you think you're going?" Courtney said.

I guess I'm so used to ignoring her, to tell you the truth, I forgot she was even standing there. "It's Saturday, remember? I'm going to D.C. like I always do."

"You're taking that much stuff with you?"

I looked down at the two suitcases, backpack and two cardboard boxes on the floor by the front door. It must have been obvious that I cleaned out my room and was leaving for good.

"You can't leave, at least not yet. Your dad wants you here when he gets back. He wants to talk to you."

"He can talk to me in D.C. I already called a cab."

"Didn't I just say he wants you here?" Courtney said, as the house phone began ringing.

"I want to go to D.C. with Kenisha," Jr. said.

"I want to go, too," Jason added. "Me, too, me, too."

"Jason, we gotta get dressed and get our stuff so we can go," Jr. said quickly, right before they turned and ran up the stairs yelling and laughing about going to D.C.

"Kenisha, your dad said for you to be here when he comes home. I'm trying not to hear him talk about how I kicked you out while he wasn't here." The phone rang again.

"I'll tell him the truth that you didn't. I'm leaving 'cause that's what I want to do."

"You need to wait for him." She walked into the living room to answer the phone. I heard her talking, then she was yelling. Apparently she'd been getting crank calls. "I hate this shit. It ain't funny."

I looked at her knowing that she probably was the one who did the same thing to my mom. "No, it's not funny. Remember that next time."

"Excuse me, are you trying to say something to me?"

I didn't answer. It was too early to get into anything with her. Besides, all I wanted to do was get to D.C. A car horn blew outside as a cab drove up in the driveway. I looked out the window. "That's my cab." I opened the front door, grabbed both suitcases and went outside. The cabbie popped the trunk, and I put them inside. I went back twice to get the two big boxes. The last time I grabbed my backpack and kind of turned to take a look around. I don't know what I was looking at or for. I guess I was just trying to remember. "Tell Dad I'll be at my grandmother's."

"We're ready," Jr. hollered as he came flying down the steps. Jason was right behind him. "We're ready, we're ready." They each had gotten dressed over their pajamas and put sneakers on. Jason's were on the wrong feet, as usual, but he was ready.

They went running past Courtney. But she moved fast and grabbed both by their collars. They squirmed and yelled for her to let go. "We want to go with Kemesh," Jason cried.

"Get your butts in this house. I just made breakfast, so get in the kitchen and eat."

"I don't want to eat. I want to go with Kenisha," Jr. said.

"Yeah, I want to go with Kemesh too."

"Go eat, now," Courtney pulled harder, turning them and maneuvering them back into the house. They stopped squirming and stopped to look back at the cab.

I was already inside, so I waved and blew them a kiss. They waved sadly, turned and went inside. I never would have thought it, but I was actually really close to my dad's other kids. It started out just to get on Courtney's nerves by getting them to do things to drive her crazy, but it soon became fun. It was childish, but I had a blast seeing her face. I was even teaching them how to swim.

* * *

The cab pulled up at my grandmother's house about twenty minutes later. I got out and started pulling my stuff out the trunk when I heard somebody behind me.

"Hey, Shorty, you're early."

I smiled without looking. I knew that it was Terrence Butler, the lawn mower guy. I still called him that sometimes 'cause that's all I knew to call him before. The first time I saw him he was mowing my grandmother's yard, and he looked so good. But aside from his body, which was slamming, LL-Cool-J hard, and his one dimple, which was too cute, I think his soft, light-colored eyes were his most attractive feature. They were warm and mesmerizing.

I turned to him and smiled even brighter. Seeing him felt like home. "Hey lawnmower guy," I said. Yep, he looked good. He was wearing a white polo with jeans and sneaks. His big biceps and triceps poked through his shirt, and I felt butterflies fluttering in my stomach. He'd gotten his hair cut off, all of it, so the natural, barely blond tips were all gone.

"What happened to your hair?" I asked, surprised.

He reached up and ran his hand over his head from front to back. "I'm pledging this semester."

"You're pledging," I said. He nodded. "I didn't know you were pledging a fraternity this year."

He started laughing and ran his hand over his bald head again. "It's hard. The big brothers are killing me."

"They made you shave your head?" I asked.

"Let's say it was highly suggested."

"Is it really crazy? Do they make you eat disgusting things like on reality shows?"

"Nah, it's not too bad. You have no time to yourself. Every waking minute belongs to the big brothers, and they can make you do anything they want," he said as he took the two boxes and a suitcase. "What's all this, you giving up on Virginia and staying this time?" he asked, jokingly.

"Yeah, as a matter of fact I am," I said.

"For real?" he asked.

"Yeah, for real," I said.

"Why, what happened?"

"I got expelled."

"From school? For what? What happened?"

"Fighting."

"Are you kidding me," he half smiled, obviously not wanting it to be the truth. "What were you fighting about?"

"Which time?" I asked. "Come on." We carried my things inside the house. My grandmother was already up, of course. She was in the kitchen cooking something. It smelled good. "Hello," I called out as soon as I entered. I waited for the petite, gray-haired woman to appear. She came from around the corner. "Hi, Grandmom," I said smiling. It was actually good to see her. Other than my sister, Jade, she was my only connection to my mother.

"Well, good morning. You're here early," my grandmother said as she wiped her hands on her apron and opened her arms wide to me. I hugged her. She felt like home and she smelled like cookies. She stepped back, looked at me, then squinted, seeing my expression. "Everything all right?"

I looked at Terrence, and he looked at me. "I'm a let you ladies talk a bit. Mrs. King, call me when you want me to check out those bushes for you. Shorty, call me, okay," he said. I nodded.

"Thanks, Terrence, I'll make sure to do that," she said as Terrence left. "Well, now, let me look at you."

"Why?" I asked, figuring she might already know what happened.

"Because you're going to be sweet sixteen tomorrow, and I want to make sure I remember you as my little girl."

Man, sweet sixteen, I almost forgot all about that, again. Funny, I waited a long time to be sixteen. Now that the day was almost here, it felt nothing like I thought it would be. "Grandmom, something happened at school that we need to talk about. It's something bad."

"Come on in the kitchen. We'll talk there."

I followed her and saw that she was right in the middle of making gingerbread cookies. There were little brown men everywhere, all over the counters and table. "What's all this?" I asked.

"Your mother loved gingerbread cookie men," she said, as she leaned over and peeked in the oven. "She told me you did too, so I thought I'd surprise you and make a few for tomorrow."

"What's tomorrow?" I asked. Duh?

"Your birthday," she said, bringing a wire rack covered with cookies to the table. She sat down and looked at me. "Come on. Have a seat and tell me this dire news."

"I don't know about dire, but it's—yeah—I guess dire is a good way to describe it. Since school started I haven't been doing so well. I'm behind in my classes, and I been kind of getting in some trouble."

She picked up a small tube of icing and handed it to me. I squeezed it, and a thin stream of white sugar poured out onto my finger. I tasted it. It was heavenly. I watched as she picked up another tube and a cookie, then began decorating. I did what she did. "Go on," she prompted.

"I got ISS, in-school suspension, for three days. Then I got into an argument with a teacher and then a couple of fights."

"You were fighting?" she asked, looking up from her busy work. I nodded. "Okay, what else?" she asked.

"The school gave me one more chance to act right and I did. I did all my current assignments and even began doing the past work, but then I got in another fight."

"Same girl?"

"No, somebody different. She thinks I want LaVon back, and I don't. Remember, I told you about all that. She's pregnant."

"Oh, your friend, what's her name?"

"Chili, and she's not my friend anymore."

"That's good to hear."

"Anyway, she pushed me and I punched her. We fought."

"I see, so tell me, what does all this mean?"

"It means that I got expelled for the semester. I can't go back until next semester. I'd have to take an entrance exam at the end of October. But right now I have to find someplace else to go. Dad wants to hire a tutor for me for the next two months, but I think I just want to go to Penn Hall."

She looked up again. "Penn Hall?" she asked. I nodded. "Do you know anything about Penn Hall High School?"

"No, I saw it a few weeks ago. Why?"

"Do you think you're up to going there?"

"It's just a high school, right? No big deal."

"Penn Hall is not just a high school. It's very different from the all-girls academy you attended. The rules are different. You're going to have to be alert every second. Now, did you discuss this decision with your father?"

"No. He stayed out all last night, and he wanted me to wait until he got in today. But I wanted to talk to you and see what you said about all this."

"Well, I say you need to stop all this foolishness and fighting. If you came here for sympathy and pity, you've come to the wrong place. I don't agree with anything you've done, and I don't appreciate you using your mother's memory to act out. I understand you're still angry about your mother. Lord knows you have a right to be, but ruining your life is no way to keep her memory alive. You need to talk, fine. Talk to me or Jade or your friends or your father. You got a lot of anger built up inside you and you need to find a way to release it," she said.

"You find you want to talk to someone neutral, fine. I'll find a counselor for you. But you need to grow up and stop acting a fool. You're not the only one who lost someone. I'll tell you like I told your mother over and over again—the choices you make now will follow you in the days to come."

"I know. You told me before."

"Well, apparently you weren't listening, were you?"

"I'm sorry," I said.

"No you're not, so don't try to pull the wool over my eyes. You're sorry you messed up and got caught. You're not sorry about what you did. That's going to happen later."

"Later? What do you mean?"

"Oh, you can pretend to be contrite all you want young lady, but your day is coming. One of these days you're going to have to step up and stop thinking only of yourself. Now have a cookie. We'll get you registered at Penn Hall Monday morning."

I bit my gingerbread man's head off. He was delicious. My cell rang while nibbling on his leg. It was Terrence. "Hey," I said.

"Lecture over?" he asked.

"Yeah, for now I think."

"Good, come out back."

I stepped out onto my grandmother's back porch and saw lawnmower guy standing with flowers in his hand. He gave me the flowers then moved aside. I smiled and laughed at the sight. He had arranged these white pieces of paper all over the grass to say happy birthday. "Aw, that is so sweet. Thank you," I said looking at the block letters. I gave him a huge hug and then kissed him. I stopped when my grandmother came out onto the porch.

"Grandmom, look what lawnmower guy did for me."

"I see. This is so sweet, Terrence, absolutely adorable. Now both of you, get down there and pick that up off my freshly cut grass."

We started laughing. My grandmother will never change. And I guess I don't really want her to.

Terrence and I spent the rest of the day hanging out together. I talked to Jalisa and Diamond and told them what I was gonna do about school. They weren't all that happy, but I knew they'd come around eventually. My dad called a couple of times, but I wasn't in the mood to ruin my day and didn't answer his call. I figured he'd call again on my birthday, and I'd deal with him then.

So after going to the movies, getting pizza and walking home, Terrence and I sat out on the front steps talking. "When are you going back to Howard?"

"Tomorrow afternoon. I have some studying to do before Monday morning. I have a huge exam and about ten chapters to read for another class."

"That sounds extreme."

"It's about par for college. They hand out a syllabus at the beginning of the semester and expect you to do the reading and keep up. There's nobody around to make you do the work. You just have to do it."

"What about your other classes? Don't you have assignments for them as well? How are you expected to get everything done?"

"You just do. Professors don't really care about other classes. They expect you to have their class assignments done."

"Do you like going to Howard?" I asked him.

"Yeah, I do. And it's not all about homecoming, although that's pretty nice, too. It's the culture of being there that I like. Since I'm pledging this year, it's a lot harder and that adds to the drama."

"I still can't believe you're pledging. How long will it take?"

"Eight weeks. I'm already four weeks in."

"Eight weeks! That's two months. That's forever. You have to keep your head shaved like that the whole time?"

"Yep, eight weeks." He reached up and rubbed his head.

"I don't know if I could do that."

"Sororities don't usually do the shaved head thing," he said. "Remember the Spike Lee movie *School Daze?*"

"Yeah, a little bit."

"Well, pledging is a lot like that movie."

"For real?" I asked. He nodded. I said to myself right then that I was gonna buy that movie to watch it again.

"So, are you ready to experience college life?"

"You mean go to Howard?" I asked. He nodded. I shrugged. "I don't know. I guess I should start doing something. I'm in eleventh grade so I hear the college clock ticking. Funny, I used to think my future would be perfect. I'd graduate from Hazelhurst, go to college then have the perfect life just like my…"

"Your mom?" he asked.

"Yeah, like my mom. But that's not gonna happen."

"You put too much emphasis on the perfect life. What's perfect for one person isn't perfect for another. You need to chill and relax with all that. Everything you want will happen in time. You gotta be patient, that's all."

"How do I know I have time? My mom didn't," I told him.

"Your mom was a nice person and I liked her, but she had problems. She had issues that she needed to deal with and maybe she couldn't. That's why she took the pills. Maybe if she talked to somebody about what was going on."

I nodded. He was right. She should have talked to somebody. She should have talked to me. I was right there the whole time. Why couldn't I help her? "I think mom still felt guilty because of Jaden, my sister Jade's father. He was hit and killed by a drunk driver. He pushed her out of the way saving her. They were right in the middle of an argument when it happened. She never got closure. I don't think she ever forgave herself for that. But there was nothing to forgive. It was an accident. Then I came along with my dad and more drama. She held on to all that drama."

"But people hold on to things all the time. I know I held on to the fact that my little brother was killed for seven dollars and fifty-three cents. I should have been there, but I wasn't," he said softly. I gazed at him seeing that he was still feeling it. "I had a test and I was studying. I heard the sirens, and I knew right then something was wrong. I ran down the street, but it was too late. I still feel…"

"That wasn't your fault, Terrence. It was that stupid fool's fault, the one that killed your brother. You couldn't have changed anything."

"Still…"

"Yeah, I know," I said, then reached over and hugged him. He wrapped his arms around me, and I felt protected, safe, like the world was fine again even though I knew it wasn't. We sat there a while just like that, holding each other feeling good. I started crying, I guess about everything we'd talked about and everything we didn't.

I leaned back and looked at him. He wiped a tear from my cheek then kissed me sweetly. "What am I gonna do now? I messed up so bad."

"You got expelled, fine. So now you take steps to fix it. You make it right."

"That's why I'm here. I'm getting my grandmother to get me into Penn Hall for the semester."

"Penn Hall? Why there? Can't you go someplace else in Virginia, like another private school?"

"I could I guess, but I don't want to. My dad wanted to hire a tutor for me for the next two months, but I didn't want that either. My mom wanted me to try Penn Hall, so I'm doing that."

"Penn Hall isn't fun and games, Kenisha. It's nothing like the place you went to."

"I know. No big deal. No uniforms, metal detectors, yeah, I get it. I'll be fine. You just jealous, that's all. There are guys at Penn Hall," I said finally smiling.

"Yeah, I'm jealous, right," he said playing it off.

"Yeah, lawnmower guy, I know you like me," I said bumping my shoulder to him and smiling like crazy.

He smiled and his dimple peeked out like it always did. He was so cute when he smiled. His light-colored eyes brightened. My stomach fluttered as usual. He made me feel so warm inside. Actually, it was more like hot inside. I knew he was gonna be my first. I just hadn't decided when we were gonna do it.

But it wasn't like he was asking or pressuring me like LaVon used to do all the time. We never really talked about sex. It just sort of never came up. "So tell me about the girls at Howard," I said.

"Uh-huh, now who's acting all jealous, all up in my business?" he said laughing.

I laughed, too. But inside I was feeling kind of funny. He went on to talk more about college life and I listened, but I was still thinking about the girls there. Terrence was a really nice guy and a seriously good catch. Any girl would be crazy not to want to hook up with him. They were there with him all the time, and I wasn't. He was seventeen and I was sixteen tomorrow, but since he'd skipped a grade in elementary school he was like light years ahead of me. How was I ever supposed to fast-forward to him? And now that I wasn't at Hazelhurst anymore, I need to stay on top of my game grades-wise or I'd lose him like everybody else in my life.

"Hey, you know what time it is?" he asked me.

I reached for my cell, but he took my hand instead. I looked at him just as his lips touched mine. Usually when we kiss it's soft and sweet, but this kiss was different. It felt real, whatever that was. But I liked it. He was holding me, and I wrapped my arms around his body and leaned in. I pressed close, wanting him to do more, but he didn't. We just kissed and kissed and kissed. His tongue slipped into my mouth, and I did the best I could to keep up with him. I swear I had no idea what I was doing, but seriously, it was nice. When the kiss ended he leaned back and smiled. "It's exactly twelve o'clock and two minutes. Happy birthday."

SIX

BFF

"Happy birthday to me, happy birthday to me, happy birthday to me, happy birthday to me."
                                        —MySpace.com

I **went** to bed swinging on cloud nine. Terrence kissed me to ring in my sixteenth birthday. So somewhere between eleven fifty-nine and two minutes after twelve, I was being kissed. Not bad. Actually, as a matter of fact it was pretty good. I was still smiling.

So now I'm getting dressed. It's Sunday morning and I go to church with my grandmother. Since Jade is back in school and my mom wasn't there, I decided that it might be a good thing for me to go. I don't mind church. I actually believe in God. I just have a lot of questions to ask Him. Yeah, my mom dying like that was definitely the first one. So I'm dressed and I get to the bottom of the stairs and Terrence and my grandmother are standing there waiting for me. I was stunned.

"What are you doing here?" I asked.

"Manners," my grandmother reminded me sternly.

"Sorry. Good morning, Grandmom. Morning, lawn mower guy," I said, using my favorite name for him.

My grandmother opened her arms and pulled me in tight. "Happy sixteenth birthday, baby girl. Oh, I guess I'd better stop calling you that, huh? Happy birthday, sweetheart."

"Thanks, Grandmom," I said, then wrapped my arms around her small frame and held her tight, wishing I was hugging my mom. Tears started to build in my eyes, so I quickly let go and stepped back.

"Happy birthday, Kenisha," Terrence said as he stepped up, kissed me quick, then hugged me.

"Thanks, Terrence. So what's all this? You're going to church with us today?"

"Yes, I am," he said.

"Tight, we'd better go or we won't find a parking space," I said.

Terrence opened the door and Jalisa and Diamond and Jade were standing on the front porch. "Surprise," they yelled. I staggered back and almost fell out. I had absolutely no idea they were gonna be here with me. "Happy birthday," they called out.

I started laughing. "What are y'all doing here?"

"It's your sixteenth birthday. Where else would we be?" Jade said as I stepped outside. I hugged her hard and long. She was my sister, and I loved her fiercely. I tried not to, but I started crying—not for who wasn't here with me, but for who was.

"Hey, happy birthday," Jalisa and Diamond said in unison.

I hugged them, too. My girls, best friends forever. I looked around at the smiling faces and felt so good. After everything, I have family and friends around me. I was just about to say something when the horn sounded. "Oh, no you didn't," I said, seeing the stretch Hummer limo parked out front.

"Come on, we don't want to be late to church," my grandmother said, locking the front door.

We all piled in the roomy limo. Ty, my sister's fiancé and mega superstar singer, was already inside the limo. He gave me a kiss on the cheek. "HB, little sis."

"Thanks, Ty," I said.

The limo drove us to church, then it was sitting there when we got out. Ty and Jade took us to breakfast at this super fancy restaurant in D.C. It was closed to everyone except for us. Then we drove around dropping everybody off. Grandmom went first. Then Jalisa and Diamond were next. They both got out at Jalisa's house. Her mom and sister, Natalie, were already standing out front waiting for us. Jalisa had called them. There were also a few girls I knew from Hazelhurst standing waiting. I got out first and received birthday hugs. Everybody else got out. Ty was, of course, an immediate hit. The girls from school were going nuts. They were getting his autograph on CDs and were asking for pictures with him. He agreed but insisted that all pictures with him include me, the birthday girl. Cell phones and digital cameras came out from everywhere.

Everybody was too impressed. I guess maybe they would be. Ty *was* a superstar. I suppose I was just too used to seeing him hanging around with the family. We left after I got birthday hugs, some cards and presents.

Next, the limo dropped Ty off at the airport. He was still on tour, but he took time off to be with me on my birthday. Now he had to get back to Atlanta for a sound check and concert that night. We said goodbye, and we waited for Jade, who walked into the private plane lobby area with him.

When she got back in the limo, we dropped Terrence off at his dorm at Howard. I swear as soon as he got out, girls were circling him like he was a superstar. They were looking at him like they could eat him up. So I jumped out to say goodbye. I kissed him in front of everybody. He understood and hugged me tight. "Hey, you got me, okay?" he whispered in my ear. I nodded assured. "Happy birthday."

"Thanks, call me," I said, then watched as he turned and crossed the quad headed to his dorm building. Girls were still checking him out. But for real, that suit did look good on him. So I got back in the limo. Jade was staring at me.

"What was all that about?" she asked.

"Nothing," I said, slightly embarrassed now. I looked out the window seeing that the driver was headed out of the Howard University area. "You're not getting dropped off here?" I asked.

"Trying to get rid of me?" Jade asked.

"Yeah, definitely," I said, knowing exactly why she was hanging around. "Okay, let's get it over with."

"Grandmom said that you got in trouble at school."

"I got into a couple of fights."

"And?" she prompted.

"I got expelled until next semester. I can go back after I take a test to make sure that I've kept up with my studies. But I don't know if I want to go back there. Grandmom said she'd enroll me at Penn Hall."

"Yeah. That part I heard," Jade said.

"You know mom was always talking about me going there at one time. I think maybe she'd be okay with it. My dad was talking about getting me a tutor for two months, but I'm not seeing that. I'll do Penn Hall. Mom wanted it, so I'm doing it."

"Kenisha, it's not about what Mom wanted. It's about what you need. Mom is gone, and nothing we can do will bring her back. The only thing we can do is respect her memory and be the best people we can be. And that doesn't mean fighting and getting kicked out of school."

"I know I was wrong to fight, but that's in the past. There's nothing I can do about it now."

"You're right. There isn't. We have to go from here. You're still grieving. You're angry. I get that. Hell, I'm angry, too. What you need to do is talk to somebody. Talk to me. I'm right here. That's what big sisters are for."

"But you have school and Ty and…"

"And I also have you. Part of growing up is venting anger the right way. Fighting isn't it. Dance. You're good, so get better. When you get mad about something, go to Freeman and kick it out."

I thought about what she was saying and realized she was right. I loved to dance, and it always made me feel better. "Okay, I will. And the next time I feel like slapping somebody, I'll call you."

"Excuse me," she said jokingly.

"You know what I mean," I said laughing. She laughed, too. So the driver dropped us off at our grandmother's house, and we chilled the rest of the day. I waited for my dad to call me, but he never did. I guess that was it for us.

seven

Penitentiary

"Whoa, culture shock, reality 101. I feel like Dorothy in *The Wizard of Oz*. This seriously wasn't Kansas anymore. It was like being dropped in the middle of the ocean and told to tread water. I could already feel myself drowning."

—MySpace.com

monday morning. It was the first day of school, again. But this time everything was different. I seriously thought I was ready, but driving up and walking into Penn Hall High gave me second, third and even fourth thoughts. There was no way I was ready for this.

See, all my life I went to Hazelhurst Academy for Girls, so it was a serious culture shock: guys walking around in school, no uniforms in sight, old everything, ugly everything, noise everywhere and metal detectors. What's up with all that? They had massive security and armed police officers.

My grandmother and I went to the main office and went through the paperwork process. Thank goodness for computers and the Internet. The school was able to acquire my full Hazelhurst transcript within seconds. They saw my grades, my awards, my accomplishments and they also saw that I'd been fighting. I knew exactly when the vice principal read the notation 'cause she looked up at me and frowned. They didn't know my mom and didn't have a clue and probably didn't care how her death affected me.

"You're seeing a counselor? Dr. Tubbs?"

"Yes. I had my first session last Thursday."

She nodded, then of course it came. She read me the riot act about rules and consequences. And just because I came from a private school I wasn't going to get any special treatment. She said that there were kids in the school that had real issues and that everyone was treated equally.

I nodded appropriately, giving her the standard I-get-it look. But the truth was I was getting scared. This was nothing like I imagined. I thought it was going to be easy because it was a public school. I was wrong.

The vice principal gave me a class roster and a map of the school. She told me that this was still first period and that the days were split with four classes each. There were blue and red days, and I'd catch on eventually. She wished me luck and with one last warning, she sent me to class.

Two minutes later, I knocked on the door and walked into English class. I gave the teacher a form, and he told me to take a seat. All eyes were on me as I found a seat in the back of the class. I sat and looked up at the board. They were studying the *Crucible* and the Salem witch trials. We did this last year, so I pretty much knew what was going on. So I'm sitting there and everybody tried to turn around to get a look at me, the new girl.

Okay, I knew it was going to be a long day after that. I suffered through the next two classes, went to my next class, had lunch and then went back to that same class. I ate alone.

My last class that day was French. They were pretty much up to what I was learning, so it was pretty good. I'd gotten all my books but didn't get a locker yet so I had to lug all this stuff home.

I was walking down the street loaded down when this girl came up to me. "Hey, you're new right?"

"Yeah, I'm Kenisha Lewis."

"I'm Cassandra Mosley, but everybody calls me Cassie. Yeah, I thought I knew you. You live around the way. You go to Freeman Dance right?"

"Yeah, you?"

"I live down the street. I've seen you and your friends dance. I don't know their names, but y'all are tight."

"Jalisa and Diamond. Diamond is really good."

"Yeah, that's it. I heard y'all dance with Gayle Harmon and her steppers sometimes. Do you know Tyrece Grant?"

"We danced with them once. It was tight. We had fun, but it is so hard. They never get tired, and their moves are perfect." I said, deliberately not answering the question about knowing Ty or hanging out with him.

"For real, that is so tight. So you just moved here to D.C.?"

"I'm staying with my grandmother. I used to live in Virginia and go to school there."

"What school? My cousin lives in northern Virginia."

"I went to Hazelhurst."

She shook her head that she'd never heard of it. "This is my house," she said. We stopped walking. "I usually walk to school. The school buses take too long. So, I'll see you tomorrow. Oh, I think I'm in your English and French class. If you need any help catching up, let me know."

"Thanks. See you tomorrow," I said and kept walking. My grandmother lived on the next block. As soon as I saw the house I felt relieved. Then I heard my name called. I knew that voice, I turned around. Li'l T came running up behind me.

"Hey, you heard me calling you girl. You ain't stop."

"Hello, I stopped, duh. I'm standing here aren't I."

"I saw you at school today, girl. You go to the penitentiary? Since when?"

"Since today," I said, walking.

Li'l T followed. "Girl, you look good. Why don't you hook a brotha up with those digits." I started laughing. "I'm serious. You and me can do this thing now that Lurch is out of the way."

"Lurch? Who's that?" I asked, then it hit me. He was talking about LaVon. I laughed harder. LaVon was tall and thin. He was six-foot-three, and I guess maybe he did do the Lurch thing, particularly since Li'l T was so short.

"Ah, but what about Terrence?" I asked.

"You ain't seeing Terrence I know."

"Why not, what's wrong with Terrence?"

"Nah, nah, chill. He aright, I guess. He's too old for you. You need some young blood. Check, I know how to treat a girl."

"Li'l T, Terrence is seventeen. I'm sixteen. We're a year apart age-wise. Besides, you need to find somebody your age."

"Nah, bump that. Them young girls too silly. I want a mature babe on my arm."

"I don't think my grandmother's seeing anybody," I joked.

"See, you wrong, messing with a brother like that. You wrong."

"I'm sorry," I said and wrapped my arm around his shoulder, "I was just playing. You know you my homeboy."

"Yeah, yeah, I got your homeboy. So, like, you in eleventh?" I nodded. "That's tight. So why don't you hook a brotha up with your girl's number."

"Li'l T, Chili is not my girl. We don't even talk."

"Nah, man. I ain't talking about that hoochie. She played out like the eighties."

"What do you know about the eighties. You weren't even born then."

"I hear things. I'm up on my old school."

"You don't even know what old school is," I said.

"I know old school, and I know Chili is past it."

"I bet," I said as we approached my grandmother's house. I stared up the path. "So wait, who were you talking about? Jalisa or Diamond?"

"Diamond."

"Diamond? Oh, please. Stop dreaming," I said. "She would make you cry and you know it." I started laughing. Li'l T was a trip. He was always into something. I walked up the path just as my cell rang. It was a text message from Terrence. *-Sup, how was sk00l?-*

"Yo, yo, hook me up. Think about it."

"Bye," I said, and waved without looking back. I got to the front door and reached for my key. My dad opened the door. Crap, I didn't even notice his car parked out front. "Hey, Dad."

"Get in here. We need to talk."

I walked into the living room and dropped my heavy book bag. My little brothers were there talking to my grandmother. As soon as I walked in, they looked up and ran to me. "Kenisha," Jr. yelled. Jason mimicked him.

"Hey Peanut, hey Butter," I said, palming their heads like I always did when they got fresh haircuts. "How you guys doing?"

"Fine," Jason said, holding on to my hand while Jr. started taking my books out the book bag.

"Mrs. King, would you please take the boys to the..."

"Hey guys, guess what? My grandmother made gingerbread men cookies the other day. I think we still have some in the kitchen."

"Yeah." They started screaming and jumping up and down. My grandmother stood up and cleared her throat. They immediately silenced, calmed down and looked at her. I shook my head and chuckled. Courtney would never be able to do that. My grandmother led the boys to the kitchen, and I stayed with my dad in the living room.

"I started at Penn Hall High School today," I said, figuring I'd get the conversation started and over with. I knew he was mad. His face was red-hot.

"Yes, I heard. And I can't believe you would do something so stupid..." he began.

Yep, I was right, he was mad.

"...what's wrong with you? First you're arguing with teachers, not doing your assignments, fighting. Now you just walk out and not listen. You're thoughtless and..."

I could not believe he was actually saying that. He called me thoughtless. Talk about being a hypocrite. *Please.* It was his stupid drama with Courtney that started all this mess from the very beginning. I don't know why he had to go there.

"...your behavior is totally unacceptable and I'm not putting up with it anymore. Courtney is right. You do act like a pampered brat..."

And she would know. She's a hypocrite, too.

"...I told you that I was getting a tutor and then you just walked out without saying a word to me. I told you to stay in the house, I called all day Saturday looking for you. Did it ever occur to you that I might have been concerned?"

"Yes, but I was supposed to come here Saturday, so I did."

"That's not the point, Kenisha. I specifically told you to be at the house when I got back."

"Dad, the only reason I decided to go to Penn Hall is because that's where you wanted me to go before, so I just figured I might as well go there now."

"But you knew I was talking about getting a tutor."

"Courtney was right. There's no need to spend all that money for a private tutor. I can go to Penn Hall for the rest of the semester then transfer back to Hazelhurst next semester. I'll keep up with my grades at Penn Hall, plus do extra work to prepare for the Hazelhurst placement exam. I can do this. I know I messed up, but it's not fair for everybody to suffer because of me."

"Kenisha, it's not about saving money. I told you to stay at the house. I meant it. I'm the parent, I make the decisions about your future, not the other way around. I'd rather you have a tutor. You don't know Penn Hall."

"But I went there today and nothing happened. I got my books and my classes, and I even met someone in my class who lives down the street. Her name's Cassie and she's nice."

He didn't say anything. He just stood there. "You're just like your mother, stubborn and obstinate. When did that happen?"

I half smiled. "Funny, she always said the same thing about me being like you."

He shook his head and sat. "I really miss her," he said.

"But Dad..." I started.

"I know, I know," he said interrupting, "if I loved her this much, then why Courtney?" He looked away, shook his head and sighed heavily. "The truth is I don't have an answer for that. Your mother and I began our relationship like an explosion. I fell in love with her the instant I saw her. She was with someone else..."

"Jaden, Jade's father. I know. I heard about the car accident."

"She never got over it. I'd hoped that I could take away some of her pain. Then after you were born, she was so happy. She had both of you with her. In the end, I don't know if anything I could have said or done would have changed things. Rehab didn't work so..."

"Wait," I interrupted. "Mom was in rehab? When?"

"She went to visit a sick friend, at least that's what we told everybody, even you. You were probably too young to remember. She was away for about six weeks. That's when you stayed here with your grandmother a while."

"I don't remember. So what happened after rehab?"

"She came back, she was her old self again—happy, fun and beautiful. Then I guess the demons returned," he said then stared away. I waited for him to continue, but he seemed lost in his memories.

"I guess it is what it is," I said.

"Yeah, I guess so," he said, then focused on me, seeming to snap out of his memory haze. "Okay, so fine. You go to Penn Hall and keep up with your grades because you are finishing your education at Hazelhurst. Barbara would have wanted it, and I do, too."

"I'm going back," I affirmed without a doubt.

Dad stood and looked down at me. He nodded and smiled. "I better get back to Courtney. She's probably worried about us."

"This pregnancy is hard on her, huh?" I asked. "I mean she's always pissed off about something. Is it hormones or what?"

"Yeah, but she's actually a very sweet woman. I do care about her."

"Do you love her?" I asked cautiously.

"I don't know. It's not like it was with your mother."

"Are you going to marry her?" I asked.

"No," he said without pause or consideration.

"So why live with her? I know she thinks she's going to marry you one day. It's not fair, not that I'm so tight with her or anything like that. It's just that it's the same thing you did with Mom."

"Your mother was the only woman for me, still is. I should have married her, but I didn't. Marrying someone else wouldn't seem right."

"She's got two of your kids and one on the way," I said. He just shook his head no, so I figured the conversation was over. We don't usually do the in-your-face, in-your-business personal thing. I mean, he stays out of my life and I stay out of his, so us talking like this was totally new. I kinda liked it.

He called the boys, and they walked calmly to the front of the house. I knew my grandmother had something to do with that. They had a napkin-wrapped cookie in each hand. The smile on their faces was outrageous. "Kenmesh, look what your grandmom gave me and Jr. We got cookies. See?" Jason said.

"Yeah, I see it, Jelly."

"Look, see, mine is almost all gone," Jr. said.

"Not bad, Bean."

"We got more, one for me and Jason after dinner and one for dad and one for mom."

"That's tight," I said.

"Thank you, Mrs. King, for everything. I appreciate this.

If there is anything you need or anything I can do, please call me." My grandmother nodded, but didn't answer. "All right, Penn Hall it is, but with serious restrictions."

"What restrictions?" I asked. He looked at my grandmother and she nodded again. I figured they had cooked something up before I got home. But I figured I'd deal with it later. I walked my dad and the boys to the car. "Dad, you forgot to wish me happy sweet sixteenth birthday."

He stopped as if cemented still. He forgot. I hoped he hadn't, but he obviously had. He turned to me, half smiled and kissed my cheek. "Happy birthday, baby."

"Thanks."

I stood waving as they drove off. So, first day of school—again—Monday wasn't all that bad. I just needed to find out what these restrictions were. I went back in the house. It was time to get started with my new life.

eight

Knock, Knock, Who's There...

"I hate stupid jokes. They're never funny."
—MySpace.com

I was kicking ass with my studies. I had my Penn Hall classes locked down tight. Actually, the classes were harder than I thought. Since it was public school, I guess I thought they were gonna be easy, but they weren't.

I was also online every day checking out my Hazelhurst classes. My student assignment-link account was still open, so I used it to stay up on what my Hazelhurst classes were doing. I had two sets of books, and every night I did two sets of assignments. It was hard, but I was handling it.

I'd been at Penn Hall for three weeks, and everything was tight. I met a few new friends and was hanging with Cassie mostly. I still hung out with Jalisa and Diamond—that wasn't going to change.

So it was last period and I was headed to my French class. I was walking down the hall and saw this crowd standing by the lockers. This girl had a PSP and all these other people were gathered around her looking at it. They were talking and laughing. I didn't stop. I just kept going. I had no intention of getting involved with new drama.

"That's her. There she is."

I kept walking.

"See, I told y'all she think she all cute."

"I heard she tried to kill somebody with a knife over this guy."

"I can see that. Look at her. You can tell she's a skank."

I had no idea who they were talking about. I know about a handful of people in this school, so whoever it was didn't concern me.

"She think she cute 'cause she had Tyrece at her party."

Okay, hard to ignore. They were obviously talking about me. But I wasn't about to deal with this. I ignored them and just walked inside the class. I sat in my seat and opened my book. Everybody else started coming in. *Crap*. I hadn't noticed that three of the girls who were outside talking were in my French class. I focused on my book as Cassie came in laughing and sat next to me.

"Hey girl, you ain't tell me you was famous," she said.

"I'm what?" I asked.

"Don't be fronting. You're famous. You're Jade's sister, right. You know Tyrece Grant. I saw you and him all hugged up on this website. He did a concert for your sixteenth birthday," she said. "When was that?"

"What? No. He didn't do a concert for my birthday."

The late bell rang, and our teacher closed the classroom door. "It's all over school," Cassie whispered continuing. "And I didn't know you were seeing LaVon Oliver," she added as the teacher started walking around handing out graded reports.

"Yeah, so? That was months ago. We broke up," I said. Actually it was only about a month ago, but for some reason it seemed like a lot longer. I guess 'cause so much had happened.

"Well, you need to be careful 'cause I heard that some of the guys were talking about getting with you 'cause you like to open your legs."

"I like to what?" I asked, completely shocked.

She held her hands up like she was surrendering. "Hey, don't shoot the messenger. I'm just giving you a heads-up. You got a rep now. The guys think you're an easy lay and the girls think you're a skank."

"Shit," I said too loudly, just as the teacher walked by. *"Excusez-moi, Mademoiselle Lewis, qu'avez-vous dit?"*

The classroom suddenly got quiet. My heart was beating a mile a minute. I don't know why I thought I could just go about my business and not sit in somebody's spotlight. *"Merde,"* I said correcting myself in French. The teacher pursed her lips, and the rest of the class laughed. In advanced French class we were only allowed to speak French, so I did.

Class dragged on for the next ninety minutes. When the bell rang, I damn near broke a record trying to get out of there. Usually I hang around and walk Cassie to her locker. Then she walks me to my locker, and we walk home together. Today, I just needed to be out of there.

So I was at my locker getting the books I needed for

the weekend, and this guy comes up to me. I looked at him and remembered Cassie's warning. Obviously this was the beginning.

"Hey, I'm Troy."

I kept stuffing books in my backpack. "Hey."

"You're Kenishiwa, right. So what are you doing this weekend?"

"Excuse me?"

"What are you doing this weekend? Maybe I can come over to your house. We can hang out."

I looked him up and down. He was cute and all, obviously on some kind of sports team 'cause he had a jersey and letter jacket on. Then I noticed these guys standing across the hall watching us. It was LaVon and his boys all over again.

"Thanks, but I'm busy this weekend," I said, closing my locker and slinging my book bag over my shoulder. I walked away.

"Hey, hey, wait. Come on. Tell you what, why don't you come over to my house then? My folks will be there, and I'll be a perfect gentleman, I swear."

"No thanks. I gotta go." I walked away barely seeing Cassie waiting for me down the hall. She was sitting on the bench at the exit, then stood when I approached.

"Damn, girl. Troy? You hanging with Troy now? Sierra is gonna freak."

"What? No. He just came up talking some crap. I have a boyfriend, and it's not LaVon."

"What school does he go to?"

"College."

"You're seeing some guy in college? How old is he?"

I glanced at her. For some reason her being all up in my business seemed odd. "His name is Terrence Butler. He used to go here."

"I remember him. He lives around the way. You're seeing him? Nice. I don't blame you for blowing Troy off and dumping LaVon."

"LaVon wasn't all that. And no we weren't together like that no matter what you heard about me."

"See, I knew all that was just talk," she said. "So what are you doing this weekend?"

"I don't know. Probably go to Howard and see Terrence," I said, knowing that I was lying. I'd never been to his dorm room, but for some reason it was important for Cassie to know that Terrence and I were tight like that.

"So tell me about Tyrece. What's he like really?"

"He's a nice guy. He's funny, but he tells the worst jokes in the world. Sometimes he comes over to the house with Gayle and his friends. We all just sit around watching TV and hanging out."

"Gayle? You mean Gayle Harmon?" she asked.

"Yeah."

"Man, I can't believe how large you are, girl. Do you know half the students in school know who you are now? You're famous."

"No, I'm just trying to get through this semester, that's all," I told her.

"Are they coming over to your house this weekend? Can you introduce me?"

"Most of the time they just show up. I actually never

know when they're coming. But I promise that next time they're at the house I will call you to come over."

"For real, for real?" she squealed laughing.

"Yeah, for real, for real."

It seemed that we got to Cassie's house quicker than usual. We stood a while and talked about our assignments. Then she went in and I started walking home. I stopped when she called me.

"Kenisha, wait, I gotta tell you something. Sierra Clark, you know her right?" she asked. I shook my head no. "Well, Sierra is one of the popular girls in school. She's on the dance team, and she was talking smack about how she can dance better than you. She also said that the only reason you were with Tyrece and LaVon is that you were giving it up. I know Sierra from when we went to elementary school. We were best friends then, but now we don't even speak mostly. Anyway, watch your back. To tell you the truth, I don't even like her."

"Thanks, I will," I said, then started walking home again. See, this is all I need—more drama. What next?

nine

Trouble…

"Ever notice how you never see trouble coming. They say you see it a mile away, but that's not true. Trouble—real trouble—just pops up right in your face. Bam!"

—MySpace.com

I WAS dancing, and it felt great. I dumped my books, told my grandmother that I'd be back and went to Freeman Dance Studio. I reserved a room on the top floor so I didn't have to deal with anybody. My real class didn't start for another hour, but I just wanted to go early and do like Jade said. I needed to dance some drama away.

So I was doing some steps Gayle and Jade taught me when I heard all this hollering and clapping. I turned around. Jalisa, Diamond and Li'l T were standing at the door watching me. I laughed and did my curtsy and bow then turned off the music and went over to them.

"What are y'all doing here so early?"

"Well, we did stop by your grandmother's house to give

you a ride, but she told us that you had already gone," Diamond said.

"Girl, you looking tight out there. You look good," Li'l T said, smiling from ear to ear.

"Yeah, but you also looked pissed," Jalisa said.

"Well, some stupid stuff…" I began then stopped, seeing that Li'l T was right up there in my business listening. I looked at him. Jalisa and Diamond looked at him.

"See, y'all wrong, I'm supposed to leave now, right?" We just looked at him without speaking. "Yeah, I know get out, right?" he said.

"Right," the three of us said all together then laughed.

"Whatever. See, y'all ain't right. I helped you find Kenisha and this is how you say thanks, by kicking a brotha to the curb." He kept on muttering as he walked away.

Jalisa and Diamond were already dressed, so we all sat on the floor as they warmed up. I told them what happened at school. They weren't all that surprised. Apparently the same rumors were going around at Hazelhurst. They said that my sweet sixteen outing with Tyrece was said to be so much better than Chili's birthday party earlier in the year. Chili was livid, of course. Now everybody wanted to know where I was so they could hang with me. Please. Talk about for-real posers.

After that conversation, we just sat talking about everything else, just like the old days. After a while we started dancing and coming up with steps. Time flew by. We did our class, then afterward sat on the front steps talking. We didn't feel like going to the pizza place, so we just chilled out in front of the Freeman building.

It was getting late. Jalisa and Diamond gave me a few copies of class assignments. I checked them out quickly and decided that they were worth doing. I walked them to the car but decided not to get a ride home. I was tired, but it was a good tired and I felt like stretching and walking.

On my way home I walked by Sierra and some of her friends. They were sitting on somebody's front steps. I had no idea if she lived there, but I made a mental note to walk on the other side of the street next time.

"Hey, you Kenisha?" I heard her even though I had my earbuds in. I kept walking like I was only hearing my music. "Hey," she tapped me on the shoulder.

I stopped and looked at her like I didn't hear her. "Hey," I said.

"You Kenisha?" she repeated. I nodded. "I'm Sierra. I heard you were talking to Troy today at school."

"Who?"

"Troy," she repeated slowly, apparently not sure if her information was accurate. She glanced over my shoulder. "Troy. Cute, football player?"

"Oh, yeah, he stopped by my locker to say hi."

"So you interested in him, too."

The word *too* got me. What was that? "No, I'm already seeing someone. He's in college."

"College?" she asked, totally not expecting that answer.

"Yeah, he goes to Howard. So, no, I'm not interested in Troy or anybody else at Penn Hall."

"Because that's what I heard," she said, rolling her neck as her girls came down off the steps to back her up and stand behind me.

I knew that scene. I'd been there before. It was about to jump off. I braced my dance bag on my shoulder wishing that I had something heavier to swing at her face, but with three of her friends behind me, I wasn't gonna get much more than one good hit anyway. I shifted my weight and took a deep breath. Ready.

"Sierra, what's up with you, girl? Why don't you back off and leave her alone. Go sit you big ass down."

New voice. Male voice. I looked around.

"Screw you, D," she snapped back instantly.

"You tried that. You messed up both times, remember?"

Whatever that meant, it hit the target. It pissed her off big time 'cause she started a string of cuss words that I swear I never even heard before. If words could kill, whoever he was would be dead, stomped, grounded, cremated and then buried six feet under plus one extra foot just because.

"What you think you gonna do?" he asked her threatening, getting out of a car parked in the middle of the street. "Why don't you back off before you get your ass hurt?" he said, more than a little threatening.

I noticed that the three girls that were behind me had suddenly gone back to have a seat on the steps again. They were acting like they weren't involved, but it was obvious that they were listening.

"Why don't you back off, D? Ain't nobody talking to your tired ass. You think you own this street? Well, you don't. Don't nobody even like you. Acting like you some big man, you ain't nothing but a punk. So you back off.

This ain't none of your business," Sierra said, rolling her neck the entire time.

Okay, I swear I felt like I was standing at Tombstone in the middle of the gunfight at O.K. Corral. They obviously knew each other and apparently they had drama issues.

"Why don't you make me, bitch?" he said angrily, stepping up to her.

Make that major drama issues.

"What you gonna do, D?" she asked equally defiant, "Hit me?" Looking at her and hearing her talk was like an oxymoron. The two didn't match. She was pretty, but her mouth was foul, plus it was like watching David go up against Goliath. She was my height and maybe even an inch shorter. He was tall and muscle-thick but not bulky. He could probably clock her with one hit.

"You think I won't," he said, as they literally came face-to-face. She didn't move an inch or bat an eye.

Okay, this was seriously my exit. I backed up and started walking away. They continued arguing so nobody said anything to me. I think I started breathing again when I was in the next block. Whatever finally happened, I really didn't care. He had thug gangster written all over his face, and she looked like she could hold her own with him. But...

"Hey."

I didn't have my earbuds in, so I couldn't pretend that I didn't hear or that the person wasn't talking to me. I stopped and turned around. *It wasn't Sierra.* "Hey," I said getting ready for anything.

"Don't pay attention to Sierra. She's all talk. She's still pissed off, that's all," said the girl approaching me.

"Yeah, I got that, but I don't know why she's pissed at me. I don't even know her or Troy."

"I think she wants to talk to Troy."

"So she should do it and stay out of my face. I don't want him. I got enough drama with the Y chromosome," I said dryly. I hadn't intended to be sarcastic, but I guess that's how it came out.

She laughed and I smiled. I think she actually understood my levity. That surprised me. Diamond and Jalisa would have gotten the reference. But Chili would have looked stumped and gotten pissed because she didn't get it.

"That's funny," she said. "I'm Ursula. They used to call me Ula, but now I really hate that name. So you can just call me Ursula."

"Hi, Ursula. I'm Kenisha. You live around here?"

"Yeah, that was my house you stopped in front of."

"Oh, I thought it was Sierra's house."

"Nah, she just hangs out there 'cause of my brother—correction—my half brother. He's a private school dropout. They used to be tight. That was him she was arguing with." I guess I must have made a face 'cause she started laughing again. "I know, they argue like that all the time. They break up then they make up."

"And now she's interested in Troy, too."

"You obviously don't know Sierra. She wants them all."

I thought about Chili. "I had a friend just like that."

"Yeah, we all do. You go to Penn right?" she asked. I nodded. "Yeah, I saw you there. So your sister's Jade." I nodded again. "She was nice. She was my dance teacher when I went to Freeman a while back."

"You went to Freeman. When?"

"A long time ago."

"You stopped?" I asked. She nodded. "Why?"

"I don't know. I keep saying that I'm gonna go back, but I guess I just never did."

"You should go back."

"Yeah, I'm thinking about it. Maybe I will. Anyway, don't worry about Sierra. She'll just roll her eyes and act all loud, but since D told her to back off, she will. There's no way she's not going to listen to him," she said, starting to walk backward.

"Thanks Ursula, I appreciate that," I said as she turned and headed back to her house. I kept walking. I noticed a car parked outside my house. The guy, Ursula's half brother, was leaning back smoking a cigarette. He watched me as I walked up. I cracked a half smile and kept on walking.

"So what, you think you gonna take all of them at one time?" he asked. "They would have kicked your ass."

I stopped. This was apparently unavoidable. "Whatever, I wasn't going down alone."

"You got guts," he said, chuckling.

I turned around and looked at him. He was fine with a capital F. "You gotta do what you gotta do, right?" I said, trying not to sound too corny.

He flicked his cigarette into the street, pushed away from the car then walked up to me. He stood too close, but just like Sierra, I didn't move an inch. "I'm Darien."

"Kenisha."

He nodded then stepped back and walked around to the driver's side of his car. I watched him. He watched me. He got in, smiled, then drove away.

ten

Common Ground

> "My equilibrium is all off. I'm off balance. Everything I thought I knew is wrong, and everything I thought I had, I don't. Family, friends, acquaintances, lovers, they're all blurry now. *I can't tell who's who anymore. Can you?*"
>
> —MySpace.com

"**who** was that?"

"Hey, Grandmom," I said walking up the path. She'd just come out of the house and sat down in her chair on the front porch. She was holding a glass of something with ice in it. "I don't know, some guy. He stopped to talk."

"What did some guy want?" she asked, suspiciously.

"What every guy wants," I said cynically, sitting down in the chair beside her. "But don't worry, I have no intention of doing anything with anybody—and that includes lawn mower guy. I'm not ready."

"Uh-huh. Many a young lady said that exact same thing. And many a young lady turned into a young mother. Saying you're not ready and a boy hearing it are two different things. They needle you, they beg, they plead and they cry. They say they're going to be there if anything happens. But two minutes of bliss isn't worth the rest of your life, especially these days. Sex is just too dangerous. Do you know about sex?"

"Yes, Grandmom."

"In my day, we didn't talk so openly about such things. Good girls kept their legs closed until they got married. And even then, good girls got in trouble. Do you know about sexually transmitted diseases?"

"Yes, Grandmom."

"Good, but I can always get you a book from the library or from the bookstore in town."

"I know about STDs," I said dryly, hoping to end the conversation as soon as possible.

"In my day, we feared getting pregnant. Nowadays you need to fear getting dead. Having sex is like playing Russian roulette. You never know what you'll get when that trigger is pulled."

"Isn't that a game?" I asked, not sure exactly what it was but knowing that I heard it mentioned before.

"It's definitely not a game. It's when you put one bullet in a revolver and spin the chamber. You put the gun to your temple. The trigger is pulled, and you have a one in six chance of the bullet splitting your head open."

"Grandmom," I said, completely stunned by her outspoken bluntness. "I can't believe you just said that."

"Believe it. Sex is no joke, and it can get ugly fast."

"I know. Chili's pregnant by LaVon. He used to be

trying to get me to have sex with him all the time. But I wasn't ready, so I didn't. Then when Mom died, I guess I just gave in. I was going to do it. I was over at his house in his bedroom when I found out that Chili was having his baby," I said. I was waiting to hear her yell, but she didn't. "I'm so glad I didn't do anything. But at school now, just because I used to go out with LaVon, some of the guys think I did."

"You can't change what people think, Kenisha. As long as you know what's true, then that's all that matters. So what about you and Terrence?" she asked.

"Lawn mower guy? I like him a lot. He makes me laugh, and he makes me feel good even when I don't feel like it. He tells me the truth, especially when I don't want to hear it."

"He's a good kid. He has his head on straight, always has. He's been in trouble before, but that's in the past."

"You don't have to worry about me and Terrence, either, Grandmom. I'm still not ready, and he's never even said anything to me about us being together like that. Truth is, I'm sure there are enough girls at Howard who would be happy to take care of him that way."

"Men can make a woman weak. They can turn her head completely around—and not for the better. I'm not saying they do it on purpose. Some do and some don't. I'm saying that all in all, they do what they have to do. I wouldn't worry about Terrence and the girls at Howard right now. He has a good heart. He'll be all right."

"A good heart? Is that how Granddad was?"

"Your grandfather was a good man, yes, and in his way

he was faithful. He was a preacher, a man of God, but he had a weakness for fast women."

"You mean he was a player?" I asked, stunned.

"Is that what you call it now, a player?" she asked.

"Yes, it means that they like playing around a lot."

"Then I guess that's what he was. A player."

"But he was a preacher. How could he do that? I mean isn't that against the Bible and God and everything?"

"Man isn't perfect, that's for sure. I'm talking about men in general, all men, but that includes women as well. Your grandfather was a good preacher, but he was also a man with weaknesses. We all have weaknesses. The point is not to let them lead us down the wrong path."

"Another recipe for life?" I asked.

She nodded and smiled. "Speaking of recipes, when are you going to start dinner? It's getting late and I'm getting hungry."

My mouth dropped open. When I started staying with my grandmother after my mom died, we made a deal that I would cook dinner on Friday nights. It all started because I was complaining about always cleaning up the kitchen after dinner. I challenged her to clean up once in a while, so she made me the deal and I gave my word. "But I thought since I was out at Freeman so late you'd cook tonight."

"Where'd you get that idea?" she chuckled.

"Fine," I said, then stood up picking up by dance bag. "Why don't we have pizza tonight? I'll order from the pizza place," I suggested, hoping to not deal with all that kitchen stuff tonight.

"You already asked me to defrost pork chops. I did.

They're in the refrigerator. I think I'd like corn and some leftover green beans with that, if you don't mind."

"Okay," I said dryly, knowing that I wasn't going to get away with not cooking a full meal tonight. "I'm gonna go clean up first, then I'll be right down." She nodded and I went in the house.

My grandmother was a trip. She had rules for just about everything, but her number one rule was keeping your word. If I said I was going to do something, she expected that it would be done. I guess that was an okay way to be. I knew I could always depend on her word no matter what because of it.

So I cooked dinner, we ate and she cleaned up the kitchen. It was worth it to be sitting watching her clean everything up, plus I was actually learning how to cook. A few weeks ago she gave me an empty notebook to write down all my recipes. I also started writing down her recipes for life. I don't know why. I guess it seemed like a good idea. And now I just kind of liked it. So I was just finished writing down how she told me to make pork chops when my cell rang. I answered even though I didn't recognize the number.

"Kenisha."

"Who's this?"

"This is Darien."

"Who?" I asked, having no idea who it was. I was just about to click off when he continued.

"Don't play with me, girl. You know who this is. I know you were waiting for me to call."

"Look, I don't know who this is, and I know I didn't

give you my number. So please don't call me again." I closed my cell. I figured it was one of those stupid guys at school trying to be funny.

"Problems?" my grandmom asked. I told her about what was going on at school and what happened after I left Freeman. I could see she was angry, but she still remained calm. "I'll take care of it," she affirmed.

"Grandmom, don't. Let me handle this. If I can't, then I'll let you know. But I can't come running to you every time I have a problem. How am I supposed to be my own woman like that?"

She walked over to me and smiled with kindness in her eyes now. "Know this, I'm always here to listen and to help. Never forget that." I nodded. She walked out and went into the living room.

I stayed in the kitchen a while. I glanced down at my cell trying to figure out who'd just called. But my thoughts were interrupted when my cell rang again. I knew the number. It was lawnmower guy. We talked for about an hour. He wasn't coming home this weekend because he was still on line for the fraternity and schoolwork was getting harder. We talked about me at Penn Hall, but I didn't tell him all that other stuff going on. I didn't want him to worry. He already had a lot going on.

It was late when we hung up. I'd gone upstairs and was sitting at my laptop playing online. Terrence sent me an instant message, so we started typing back and forth while. We signed off around one o'clock in the morning. Talking to him, then IM-ing was the perfect ending to my crazy day.

Saturday, the next morning, my dad showed up early.

I was still in my room when my grandmother called me down. "Good morning, Grandmom," I said, having taken the back stairs directly to the pantry off the kitchen. "Hey, Dad, what are you doing here so early?" I asked.

"Hey, baby girl," he said, standing and kissing my forehead. "I have something for you."

"What?"

"It's in the living room. I just got them in and thought you'd like one."

We walked into the living room and there were two identical boxes sitting on the coffee table. I immediately took them off and set them on the floor. In each box was a computer conference call system. "Get out, for me? Thank you," I said.

"You're welcome. I bought five. I dropped two off to your friends Jalisa and Diamond. You are still friends this week, right?" He chuckled. I laughed and swatted at him. "I just wanted to make sure. So you go on and put it together. The instructions are easy enough. Enjoy."

"Wait, there are two of them. Who's the other one for?"

"You mentioned that you made a friend at Penn Hall."

"Oh, Cassie, right, okay." I shrugged not even thinking about her. She was okay and we walked home from school every day and all, but she was acting strange lately, like she was jealous or something. She reminded me a lot of Chili, two-faced. There was no way I was giving her this. But I knew exactly who I was giving it to.

"Listen, I gotta get to work." I smirked. He must have seen my expression 'cause he called me on it. "I'm doing right," he whispered as he kissed my forehead.

"Thanks, Dad, for real, and before you ask, I'm on top of my studies at Penn Hall and at Hazelhurst. Jalisa and Diamond have been helping me out with the assignments."

"Good girl. I'll talk to you next week. Stay out of trouble."

"I will." I walked him to the front door and watched as he got to his car. That's when it hit me. "Dad, wait," I called out and ran to him. "Wait, you said you got five. Who's the other one for?"

"I thought you might want to chat with your sister. But your grandmother told me that Jade already had something like that. So I thought I'd keep one at the house, just in case you might want to see your old man or the boys."

"Good idea." I hugged him hard, "Thanks, Dad." I stood watching as he drove off. Then, coming from the opposite direction, I saw the same car from the guy last night in front of Ursula's house. It was her brother. It hit me that he was the one who called me. *Merde.* How the hell did he get my cell phone number?

He stopped the car, and Ursula hopped out. "Hey," she said, closing the car door and walking over to me.

"Hi," I said, and then looked at her brother. He eyed me and nodded. I shrugged indifferently. "What's up?"

"Nothing," she said starting to walk toward my house like we were best friends or something. I walked with her. She was obviously pissed about something. "Sorry, he was getting on my nerves, and I was just tired of hearing his crap. I saw you standing there, so I told him I was going to hang out with you."

We walked up onto my front porch and stood looking

down the street. His car was long gone, but we kind of looked anyway. "You don't get along with your older brother?" I asked.

"Half brother," she noted emphatically. "We have the same mother, that's all. He gets on my nerves. He just got back and already he's into something. I told my mom, but she thinks the sun shines on his ass daily. They're both a trip. I swear I can't wait to go to college and get away from them."

"Sounds like fun," I said, sarcastically.

"Tell me about it," she said, equally sarcastic.

"I think he called me last night."

"You gave him your phone number? Don't tell me you're thinking about hanging with him now," she said, looking at me like I'd just killed a dozen puppies.

"No, for real no. I don't even know how he got my cell number. Nobody around here has it except Cassie."

"Then that's how he got it."

"Cassie gave him my cell number? Why? For what?"

"Probably 'cause he made her. He makes the girls around here do all kinds of things for him. He's a serious straight-up user, and I'm not saying that 'cause I can't stand his ass. For real, he's bad."

"Well, when he called I had no idea who he was. I didn't remember when he told me his name. So I kind of hung up on him."

Ursula burst out laughing. "Ohhh, I love it. You are a trip. I bet that's the first time any girl ever hung up on his ass." She continued laughing. I just smiled and looked down the street.

"Kenisha, are you ready for breakfast?" my grand-mother said as she opened the screen door to the front porch. "Oh, I didn't realize you had company."

"Grandmom, this is Ursula. She lives down the street."

"Hi, Mrs. King," Ursula said.

"Good morning, dear. Would you like to join us for breakfast?"

"Um, uh-huh, yeah," Ursula said, quickly.

"Um, uh-huh, yeah?" my grandmother repeated sternly.

I was so embarrassed. "Grandmom, she means…"

"There's nothing wrong with her mouth, Kenisha. I'm sure Ursula can speak for herself. Ursula, in this house we speak properly. Yeah, uh-uh, dis, dat and de odder won't work."

"Yes, Mrs. King," Ursula said smiling, immediately changing her tone and straightening up.

"You girls come on in, wash your hands and set the table."

We followed my grandmother back into the house. "How did you know my grandmother's name was King?" I whispered.

"Girl, everybody knows your grandmother. She's been living around here since the dawn of time." We started laughing.

After we set the table, we sat down, said grace and ate. Breakfast was good, as usual. Ursula ate like she'd never had food before. It was a good thing my grandmother cooks like crazy 'cause she had like three servings. Ursula and I cleaned up the kitchen then sat around talking. We talked about school and our classes and the teachers. We talked about the different places we hang out including the pizza place around the corner from Freeman.

"So how long you been dancing?" she asked.

"Since I was four years old."

We talked about my sister and Ty, then after a while she told me about her family. Her mother worked two jobs and was never home, and her father was in prison. She usually cooked, cleaned and took care of herself and the house. She mentioned her brother and how his being at the house was hell for her.

"Where does he go when he's not at your house?" I asked.

"He stays with his dad most of the time.

"How old is he?"

"He's seventeen. We were born fifteen months apart."

"I'll be seventeen the beginning of summer."

"Does he go to Penn Hall, too?"

"Nah. He dropped out of school a year ago. He's supposed to go back to get his GED like he promised my mom, but he's not doing anything about it. Typical."

"Where's his dad?"

"He lives in Maryland. His dad used to be a Redskins football player. That's how my mom met him. She was hanging out, and they had a thing for a while. But it didn't last. She said he was nothing but trouble. But if you ask me, that's all Darien is—trouble. He just got his ankle bracelet off."

"He had an ankle bracelet, like for house arrest?" I asked. She nodded. I shook my head. I never actually heard of anybody having house arrest before. As tough as LaVon pretended to be, he was nowhere near getting in that much trouble.

We talked about families some more, but I wasn't in the mood to share so she did most of the talking. It was like she was waiting for someone to come along to hear her drama. I felt like I should have a bust of Freud sitting over my shoulder like Tubbs.

When it was almost lunch, we went outside and sat on the front porch. We were talking about music we liked when Darien drove by in his car. "That's a nice car," I said.

"His dad gave it to him for getting off house arrest."

"What?"

"Girl, please, you don't know the half of it. He gets everything he wants. All he has to do is ask his bank. I'm not jealous or anything, but I'm just saying that's ridiculous."

"Yeah, it is kind of wrong," I said. "So why was he on house arrest?"

"Who knows? Whatever, I know that he went to youth detention a few years back for stabbing somebody," she said. I immediately thought about Terrence. He was in youth detention, too. "He got out and went back in almost immediately. After that he just kept getting in trouble."

"Typical bad boy."

"Drama is more like it. But I'm just warning you up front. I did the same thing for the others, but don't nobody be listening to me." Her cell phone rang just as she was about to say something more. She answered.

She talked a few minutes then agreed to something. As soon as she closed her cell, her brother drove up. "You gotta go?"

"Yeah, he's picking my mom up from work, but he doesn't know how to get there. I'll see you later."

"Okay, see ya," I said. When she left I started thinking about her brother. He was cute and all, but he was too far out of my league. I never met anyone who got into so much trouble.

I spent the rest of the day chillin' not feeling like doing any homework. I hung out in the garden with my grandmother until late then stayed in my room installing the new software in the computer. Sometime after dinner my cell rang, it was that number again. I answered. "Hello."

"Yeah, you know me now, right?"

"Hi," I said, not particularly impressed that he called me again, although he did have a nice voice. To hear him talk, you wouldn't think he was all drama, but apparently he was.

I asked him about his bracelet, and he told me that he got it by getting into a fight. I told him that that's what got me kicked out of private school.

"I didn't think you were from around here," he said.

"Virginia isn't on the other side of the universe." He laughed. I smiled. It was a nice laugh. I wondered if everything Ursula told me about him was true. She did sound kind of jealous. I mean his dad had all this money and he was living large and all, kinda like I was before.

"So what about your dad?" he asked.

"He played professional football then retired and opened a computer company. He's all right."

"For real, my dad played football, too. They probably played against each other. That's tight."

"Yeah, maybe," I said cautiously.

"That's tight. I never met anyone who was kinda like me. I mean our dads and all. It's kinda nice," he said. "What do you think?"

"About what, knowing somebody whose dad played football?"

"Yeah," he said.

I knew what he wanted to hear, but I wasn't ready to reach that conclusion. Yeah, we had a lot in common on the surface, but he was still too far over the top for me. "It's a'ight, I guess."

"You playing now," he joked, "so why don't we hang out?"

"Probably not a good idea," I said, knowing for damn sure that it was a really, really bad idea. But I was still tempted. He really seemed nice, and we did have that thing with our dads in common.

"Why not?"

"Aren't you seeing somebody, like Sierra?"

"Nah, she still all up in my face though, but she over. She just won't let go. For real, she's too erratic for me. I'm tired of her drama. I'm looking for somebody sweet. You know anybody like that?"

"Not really," I said, trying not to giggle, but it slipped out anyway. He laughed, too.

"A'ight, a'ight, so think about it," he said.

"Yeah, okay, I gotta go."

As soon as I hung up, I took a deep breath. I had no idea what I was doing. But talking with Darien was fun. He kinda understood me, and he listened. Maybe talking to him was okay. Maybe he wasn't all that much trouble.

eleven

Holdin' On

"An open scab takes forever to heal, especially when you pick at it. The more you pick the uglier it gets. I thought it would be cathartic to believe that all good things come to those who wait. Naive much? My bad."

—MySpace.com

Another day behind me, I marked it off on my computer calendar. I checked everything I needed to get done this week. I messed up by not doing a reading assignment and trig worksheet over the weekend. But I figured I could catch up quickly enough. The thing was not to fall too far behind.

All in all the weekend was good. After hanging out with Ursula then talking with Darien on Saturday, and then going to church on Sunday, I finished uploading my conference call software to my laptop. It was working perfectly. The first thing I did was call my girls to make sure that they were on board. They were. So using the laptop,

I talked face-to-face with Jalisa and Diamond. We had a great time. With the split screen, it was like they were right there in my room with me.

I tried to get in touch with Jade, but she wasn't around all weekend, so I left her a message with my code so that she could give me a call. I also text-messaged Terrence. I knew he was busy with his classes, plus being online was probably really tough, so I figured I'd hear from him in a few days. My grandmother was right. There was no need worrying about what he was doing or with whom. There wasn't anything I could really do about it anyway. Besides, I trusted him.

So now I'm sitting in class pretending to pay attention. The class had just finished the *Crucible* and they were discussing current ramifications of a totalitarian society. I was busy doing my trig worksheet.

"Ms. Lewis, do you want to weigh in on this discussion, or is this class boring you today?"

Hearing my name called, I looked up. *Merde, I got caught.* Again. "Huh, what was the comment?" I asked, as a couple of students in the class turned around to look at me as others laughed.

The teacher, at the front of the classroom, was looking directly at me. He crossed his arms over his chest then leaned back against his desk. "Would you please pass that paper up front to me now?"

I sighed and rolled my eyes. *Merde.* It wasn't that I couldn't get another worksheet. I could. And it wasn't that I couldn't duplicate my answers. That wasn't a problem. It's that this wasn't the first, second, third or fourth time I'd gotten caught doing Hazelhurst work in this class. Reluctantly, I passed my trig assignment to the front of the class. The teacher took it, read a few of the calculations then frowned at me. "Trigonometry. Do you have this class?"

"No, it's just something I do," I said coolly.

"You systematically work college-level complex calculations for fun? Just something you do?" he asked. Now all the students were looking at me like I had three heads. There was no real answer to the question, so I decided to let him have this round. I shrugged.

"Trigonometry is a very difficult subject, and you find it fun? What is it, like Sudoku for you?" he asked, then glanced down at the worksheet again.

I could tell he was trying to figure out something, maybe one of the problems. I smirked. I could also see he was stumped. "Yeah, sometimes," I said. Some of the students snickered and laughed. He looked around then back at me. "Since this class is obviously boring and you find trig a more stimulating distraction, why don't you spend the rest of the class time in ISD."

Finally, a break. In-school-detention was exactly what I needed to catch up on my Hazelhurst reading assignment. I got my note and went to the ISD room. As soon as I walked in, I smiled. Ursula was sitting in the back of the room.

I gave the teacher assigned to the room the note and then took a seat next to Ursula. "What are you doing here?" I asked.

"Me? You're the Goody Two-shoes. What are you doing here?"

"I got caught doing some other assignment in class."

"What? You got sent here for that? What kind of class work was it?" she whispered.

I smiled and chuckled. "Trigonometry in English lit class."

"Trigonometry? Who's class is that?" she asked.

"It's from my old school. I like to keep up with them."

"Girl, you know you are getting weird, right?" she said, laughing. I laughed too then we both straightened our faces when the teacher looked back in our direction and cleared her throat.

"So what exactly are we supposed to be doing in here?" I asked.

"Contemplating our behavior and doing class work, I guess."

"So what are you doing in here?"

"My stupid brother called me and my cell rang. He's such an asshole. I told my teacher that it was my watch, but she didn't believe me. So since she couldn't find a phone on me, she sent me here."

"That's so dumb. They sent you out of class because a cell phone rang."

"My idiot brother called like he had nothing better to do. He knows I'm in school."

"Maybe he forgot," I said, finding myself defending him.

"Oh, please," she whispered. "Don't even try it."

"All right, ladies, this isn't a social gathering. You have work to do. Let's get started," the room monitor said.

Ursula and I pulled out our class assignments and actually began doing our work. I had no idea what kind of student she was. I guess I presumed she was like her brother, but when I glanced over at her desk, her class book and notebook were open and she was working on chemistry equations. She was knocking them out like they were simple elementary school additions. Maybe she wasn't like her brother.

I began reading a Hazelhurst assignment, figuring the room monitor wouldn't have any idea what I was doing anyway. As long as I was quiet I'd be fine. I was wrong. When the bell rang, she asked to see my English work. I didn't have anything for her. I told her I was reading, but she didn't buy it. She gave me a slip for afterschool detention.

So the rest of the day wasn't too bad. I actually paid attention and did the work I was supposed to do. Then, after school I went back to detention. My English teacher was talking to the monitor. I went and sat down. He walked over and placed an assignment on my desk. It was for another book.

"Can I presume you've read this book as well?" he asked. I nodded. "Okay, why don't you tell me what class books you read last year for school?" I listed the tenth grade books to the best of my memory. He nodded each time, seeming impressed by the list. "Okay, so since you're pretty much past the rest of the class and sitting in my class is literally boring you, why don't I assign you a different syllabus? I looked over your English transcripts for this year. You were reading Greek poetry? *Lysistrata?*" I nodded. "Why don't we keep with that? I'll bring in a few assignments tomorrow. In the meantime, I want you to work on this."

I looked at the paper he gave me. It was poetry. I had

to analyze, write questions and answers then explain it as well as give examples. "Fine." He went back speaking with the monitor. I started the assignment. I barely finished when the monitor told me that detention was over. Fine, I did my time. When I finally left the building, I was so ready to be out of there. As soon as I got outside, I opened my cell and called Terrence to vent. I knew he'd understand.

"Hey, what up?" he said, after answering on the second ring. He seemed rushed and in a hurry.

"Nothing, I just needed to talk," I said.

"What's wrong?" he asked.

"When are you coming home?" I asked.

"This weekend, I hope. Why, what's going on?"

"Nothing. I just now got out of detention."

"Detention? What are you doing getting detention?"

"Stupid teacher got pissed 'cause I was doing trig in his English class. I already knew the stupid book the rest of the class was doing. I read it last year at Hazelhurst. It's like going over the same stuff a million times."

"Sometimes you just gotta deal," he said plainly.

"Deal? Nah, it was boring, so I started doing my trig work."

"You know you can't do that. There's no way you'd do that at Hazelhurst, would you?"

"I wouldn't be bored at Hazelhurst."

"You can't just play this off like it's a game, Kenisha. This is for real. If you want to go back to private school, you need to keep your grades up and stay out of trouble."

He was going on about everything he thought I needed

to do and not once did he even sound like he was on my side. "You know I called you 'cause I thought you'd be on my side."

"I am on your side," he said.

"Don't sound like it."

"I'm only telling you what you already know. You were wrong, and you know it."

"That's not the point, and besides, now the teacher wants to give me additional assignments in class."

"Good," he said.

"What do you mean good? I don't need extra work. I'm doing my class work at Penn Hall plus keeping up with the work at Hazelhurst. I think that's enough. I don't need more."

"Consider it a challenge. Look, I got class in about two minutes. I gotta go."

"Yeah, a'ight go, bye," I said, hanging up and not giving him a chance to say goodbye. I seriously didn't need to hear his drama. I expected him to be on my side. Instead he was siding with them. I crossed the parking lot but stopped when I recognized a car parked on the far side. It was Darien. He got out when he saw me coming. "Hey," he said, leaning on the hood.

"Hey," I said, not in a great mood.

"Come on, I'll give you a ride."

I looked at him standing there smiling. He was tempting, and I was pissed after dealing with the English teacher, detention and Terrence. Talking to him was a total waste of time. So not thinking, I said sure and got in the car. I sat there as he drove. The music was loud, but the windows were up all the way. I rested my head back on the soft leather and tried to relax. There was something about being here that made me uneasy. Maybe it was the whole idea that Darien was who he was or how he was.

"How'd you know I was staying after school today?"

"I hear things," he said, cryptically.

"Like what?"

"Your mom died," he said, totally taking me off-guard.

"Yeah, so?" I said easily, trying to sound like I wasn't fazed by his remark.

"You're hanging with TB."

"Who?" I asked having no idea who he was talking about.

"Terrence Butler."

"What about him? You know him?" I asked. He didn't answer.

"I also heard that you used to kick it with LaVon Oliver."

"Don't believe everything you hear."

"You weren't with LaVon?"

"Yeah, we hung out for a while, and then it was over. He calls, but I never look back," I said, trying to sound like I got it like that. We stopped at a traffic light, and I saw a couple of girls on the corner staring at the car. I could see them, but they couldn't see me 'cause the glass was smoked so dark. "So who are you hanging with now?" I asked, curiously, "Sierra?"

"Told you, nobody," he said, looking at me smiling. He had a nice smile. "I'm tired of dealing with all her drama. She may be seventeen, but she still act like a kid. She calls me all the time, always on my case wanting to talk."

Just as he said that, my cell rang. I pulled it out and looked at the number. It was LaVon. I started laughing. Darien looked at me. I shook my head. "It's LaVon. We need to introduce him to Sierra so they can both get a life and stop calling." We laughed. It was funny, something else we had in common.

I started talking to him about school and what happened earlier. He got it. He completely understood. Why Terrence couldn't be like that, I have no idea. We started talking about other things as we drove around. It took twenty minutes to get to my grandmother's house. We took the long way home.

When we pulled in front of the house, I felt weird about just getting out like that. Talking to Darien was kind of nice. He really understood me. I grabbed my bookbag and started to open the door. "Wait," he said.

I stopped and turned around. Just as I did, he leaned over and kissed me. It was hard, like he really meant it. He pulled my waist to his body and held me while we kissed. When it was over, I moved back to my side of the car. I started to leave again. "You taste good," he said, holding my hand.

I smiled and then got out of the car. Luckily nobody was out. So no one saw me getting out of his car. By nobody I mainly meant my grandmother. She'd probably have a fit.

twelve

Guaranteed Happy Ending?

> "It's a miscarriage of reality to tell children fairy tales that promise a bright and wonderful world. It's when we grow up that we find out the world isn't all glass slippers and royal balls. It's more like curses and poison apples."
>
> —MySpace.com

It was Friday morning. There was no school because of a teacher workday. I got up early, ate, then went back to my room and took the online Hazelhurst admissions exam. It was much harder than I thought, but I think I did okay. I guessed I would find out the next week when the results would be mailed out. I felt like a heavy burden had been lifted. I stressed for days over the test. Now I'm just glad it's over with.

Lawn mower guy was supposed to come home this weekend. I waited all day for him to show up, but he didn't. He does this a lot. I guess what he's got going on at school is more important than hanging with me.

Whatever, I still can't believe that I trust that he's going to do like he says. I finally gave up waiting and went to dance class to chill out.

Jade was right. Going to Freeman and dancing was the best therapy in the world, particularly after taking the exam. Who needs Tubbs and Freud when I have tap, ballet, hip-hop and jazz? Seriously, dance is the one thing I can always count on in my life.

After an hour and a half of dancing, I was exhausted. Neither Jalisa nor Diamond came, so it was just me and a few others in class. I was walking home again afterward, listening to my music and taking my time. I saw Darien's car parked out front of Ursula's house. I also saw Sierra sitting on Ursula's steps talking on her cell. I was walking on the opposite side of the street, so it was cool. I wouldn't have to deal with her. It was obvious that we weren't going to be best friends. So ignoring her seemed the best course of action.

Out the corner of my eye I saw Darien get out of his car. He was talking to somebody on the phone. I half smiled supposing that it was Sierra, but she kept on talking on her cell. He ended the call then turned when he saw me coming. He crossed the street to stand a few feet ahead of me then waited. At least he knows I'm alive and gives me some attention, unlike some people. He was smiling when I walked up to where he stood. "Hey, you here to see me?" he asked knowing better.

I knew he was joking. I pulled one of my earbuds from my ear and glanced over, seeing Sierra staring me down. "Nah, sorry," I said, still walking.

"Hey, hey, hey, wait up. I just want to talk to you. Why don't you get in the car, and I'll give you a ride."

"I live up in the next two blocks. I can walk."

"I didn't say I'd take you home. I said I'd take you for a ride. Come on, get in."

I looked at his car. It was seriously nice and riding inside was like sitting on a cloud. But I knew Sierra, still sitting there, would pass out. So, do I rub it in her face that Darien was taking me out in his car, or do I skip all the drama and pass? I decided to skip the drama and pass. "Nah, that's okay. I need the exercise," I said putting my earbud back in my ear.

"You sure?" he asked. I nodded. "Okay, next time."

I waved and kept walking knowing that he was still watching me. Sierra, too. I didn't change my pace but I kept on walking. I saw Ursula walking, coming in my direction. I smiled and stopped, pulling my earbuds out. "Hey, your grandmother told me you were at dance class," she said. "I was just going over there."

"Yeah, I was," I said, "What's up?"

"Listen, today's my mom's birthday, and she decided at the last minute to throw herself a birthday party. Want to come?"

"Tonight?" I asked, surprised about the short notice.

"Yeah, it's no big deal, really. She found out that she got the night off work, and she wanted to do something. Plus she was talking about doing something to welcome Darien home again. Her friends will be upstairs, and we'll be downstairs. It's just going to be kids from school and around the way. It's no big deal really, but you should come, for real."

"I don't know. My girlfriends might be stopping by."

"Bring 'em."

"Are you sure?" I asked.

"Yeah, it'll be fun."

"Okay," I said and started walking.

"Wait, you gotta see this outfit my mom just got me. Come on. I'll show you. I think I'm gonna wear it tonight," she said excitedly, turning me around facing her house. Darien was leaning against his car watching us talking, but he was on his cell again. Sierra was nowhere in sight.

I walked with Ursula back to her house, climbed the front steps and went in. Her house was bigger inside than it looked outside. There was a woman in a T-shirt and jeans wiping a huge mirror in the living room over the sofa. "Mom, this is Kenisha. She's Mrs. King's grand-daughter from down the street."

"Hi, happy birthday," I said. Then it hit me, I had no idea what I should call Ursula's mom. Ursula's last name was Dean and Darien's last name was Moore.

"Hi, Kenisha, thank you. Are you coming to Darien's party tonight?"

"Yes, I think so."

"Come on, it's upstairs," Ursula said.

"Ursula, did you vacuum that downstairs like I told you?"

"You told Darien to do it."

"I told *you*," her mother insisted.

She looked at me and rolled her eyes to the ceiling. I knew the feeling. Housework wasn't exactly my favorite thing to do either. "I'll do it after I show Kenisha my new outfit."

Darien walked into the house and stood in the living room, "Do it now, Ursula. I don't want this place looking like a pig sty tonight. Darien can show Kenisha to your room. Then he's going to drive to the store and pick up a few things for me."

"Fine," she huffed, "I'll be right back."

"Darien, show Kenisha to Ursula's room."

He smiled and headed up the stairs. I followed. From what I could see, there were four bedrooms upstairs. Darien went to the one at the back of the house. As soon as I walked in I could tell that it wasn't Ursula's bedroom. I stood in the doorway. "Come on in," Darien said. "I just need to change so I can go to the store." By the time he finished the sentence he had already taken off his shirt. I stood there looking.

He had a nice body. I guess I wasn't exactly surprised, but I, for real, never thought about it. Whenever I think about a guy's body, I think about lawn mower guy and the first time I saw him at my grandmother's house. Remembering him standing at the shed still put a smile on my face.

"Why don't you come in," Darien said.

Okay, the last time I was in a guy's bedroom is when I foolishly decided that I was going to give LaVon my virginity. It didn't happen, but I did find out that he was seeing my ex-friend, Chili. Why do all guys' bedrooms look alike? Just like LaVon, Darien had big gaudy trophies everywhere. It was like they were trying to prove their manhood by displaying them. "No thanks, I gotta go. Tell Ursula that I'll see her later." I turned to leave.

"You coming tonight?" he asked, walking to the open door.

I shrugged, him standing there with his shirt off started to make my stomach tingle. "Maybe, I'll think about it," I said.

"You should come."

He was too close. I looked away then down, seeing a big scar on his shoulder. "What happened? How'd you do that?"

He started laughing. I looked at him. It was like I just told the funniest joke ever. "What's the joke?" I asked.

"Ask your boy," he said offhandedly, smiling cryptically.

"My what?" I asked.

"Darien, Mom wants you downstairs. She has her list, and she wants you to go to the store now," Ursula said, coming up behind me as I stood just outside Darien's bedroom door. "Come on, Kenisha."

I gave him one last questioning look then followed Ursula. We went into Ursula's room two doors down from Darien's. It was closest to the stairs, and she left the door open. I sat on the bed with my back to the open door and grabbed a magazine that had been tossed on the floor. I waited as Ursula pulled out a couple of shopping bags and began pulling clothes out. She held up a shirt smiling. "What do you think?" she asked.

"I like it," I said. I did, 'cause I bought one just like it a few months back. She pulled out another two shirts, a pair of jeans and a jacket. They were all nice, but I really wasn't paying much attention anymore. Darien said something about one of her shirts while standing in her doorway. He and Ursula started talking. Well, more like bickering. Then she told him to shut up and get out of her room. She turned her back to hang up the jacket. I knew Darien was still there, and I knew he was looking at me.

I started flipping through the magazine, trying not to pay any attention to him. A few minutes later I heard Ursula's mom calling to Darien. He walked away, and then I heard him talking downstairs. I exhaled slowly. Him standing behind me like that was starting to make me nervous. I don't know why.

Anyway, Ursula was talking about how much she liked shopping but how all the stores around the way were old and tired. She went on talking about seeing two or three girls at school with the exact same outfit on. She asked me where I shopped for my clothes. I told her about the shopping mall not far from my dad's house, my old house. I told her the next time I go shopping, I'd let her know. She seemed happy about that.

So we talked about what she was going to wear tonight and who might show up. I asked her if Cassie would be there. She seemed sure she would be since the party was pretty much open to everybody who wanted to come.

"Is Sierra coming?" I asked.

"I don't know, but probably."

"I saw her sitting on your steps earlier. I guess she was waiting to talk to you."

"I don't know why. We're not exactly good friends anymore. We used to be kind of close, but after she got pregnant last year she turned all attitude. She was probably waiting to talk to Darien."

"She's pregnant," I asked, surprised. I don't know why I was surprised. Nothing should really surprise me anymore.

"Not now. Last year, but she miscarried. But yeah, girl, Darien Jr. She almost had a paycheck with Darien's face stamped on it for real."

I started laughing, "Darien almost a dad," I said.

Ursula nodded. "Actually he is a dad, but I don't know the other girl and never even saw the baby. I think she lives around his dad's place. That was two years ago. Believe it or not, they're still fighting over child support and DNA. See, he's just plain old drama."

"Wow."

"Yeah, tell me about it."

"He told me that Sierra calls him all the time bugging him. So they're still together, right?"

"Nah, hell no. After she got pregnant, he broke up with her. Talk about not manning up. So typical. He's such a triflin' ass. Instead of stepping up to his responsibilities, he turned his back on her."

"No wonder she's pissed off at him."

"Tell me about it. Anyway, now that he's off house arrest, I guess she'll be hanging around again."

"So why exactly was he on house arrest?"

"He beat some guy up right outside of school. They say he even stabbed the guy, but not seriously. The police said that it was drug related, but nobody found any drugs on him. Sierra was there when it happened. She covered for him saying the other guy jumped Darien with a knife. Everybody knows she'd lie for him. She probably hid the knife and drugs to cover for him."

"You think it was drug related, too?"

"I wouldn't be surprised. Darien is so dumb. With his

dad's money and help, he could be doing anything and be anything. Instead he's hanging around playin' gangsta and getting in trouble acting like some street thug. Then when he gets in trouble, his dad bails him out. That's so wrong. Money is privilege."

"Not all the time," I defended weakly.

"Name one time it's not. Darien could go to school and be anything he wants. Instead he does the, 'I'm pissed at the world' thing and gets away with murder, literally."

I didn't say anything. That kind of used to be me, too. My mom and dad used to bail me out all the time, too. Once I got caught shoplifting. When my parents came, they paid a fine and I got off. I was so scared. I never, ever did it again. "Really?"

"Before that, when he was younger, he tried to rob this kid. They got into a pushing thing. The kid got stabbed and D went away. He's got serious anger issues when he doen't get his way."

"Really," I repeated, "but he's so nice."

"Yeah, but he's got a bad temper. He fights all the time."

"Don't we all," I said knowingly. "I gotta get ready to go. I have stuff to do before tonight. I'll see you later." She said okay and I left. Truth was I realized that Darien and I were so much more alike than I thought before, definitely more than lawn mower guy and me.

I got back to my grandmother's house. She was on her way to Friday night bingo at the church, but she sat a while to talk with me. I told her about the party at Ursula's house. She wanted to know about adult supervision. I told her about Ursula's mom having her birthday party upstairs. So she said I could go. After she left for bingo, I called Jalisa and Diamond.

"I took the exam this morning," I said.

Both Jalisa and Diamond screamed, and then they started asking all these questions about it. "Yes, it was hard. It's a lot like the SATs and ACTs. Each section was timed, and if you didn't finish, the computer screen would just shut off on you. There were no breaks. The test lasted two hours. I'll get a letter of my results next week." After all the questions were asked and answered, we didn't say anything more about it.

"Okay, enough exam talk. I need to chill. Y'all want to go to a party tonight? Then y'all can spend the night and we can go to Saturday dance class from here tomorrow."

"Where?" Diamond asked.

"Yeah, I don't care. Where?" Jalisa said eagerly.

As usual Jalisa was all for it, but Diamond was the conservative one. She was the one who thought about everything she did before she did it. Jalisa and I were more spontaneous. I guess that's why we stayed in trouble more than Diamond. So I started telling them about Ursula, Cassie, Sierra and Darien. But I didn't tell them about the kiss. I still couldn't believe it myself.

Six hours later, after getting dressed at my place, we started walking down the street to the party. We were talking about Freeman and Hazelhurst as usual. Then Diamond prompted Jalisa to tell me her big news. "What? What?" I said. "Tell me."

"I'm kind of seeing Isaac," she said.

"Well, it's about time. You've been dragging that guy's picture around for what, four years now."

"Ohh, see, that's exactly what I said," Diamond laughed and joked. "See, I told you."

"Yeah, whatever," Jalisa said. "I admit it, he's nice."

"I know he's one of LaVon's boys, and they hang out and all, but you know he's nothing like LaVon," I said. We all agreed. "First of all, he's the only one who actually has a good shot at getting in the NBA, not bonehead LaVon." We busted out laughing. "I swear I have no idea why I was dealing with the fool."

"So how's lawn mower guy?" Diamond asked.

"Absent," I said.

"What do you mean, absent?"

"He was supposed to be hanging out with me this weekend, but he bailed. He does that a lot lately. I guess it was schoolwork again. But seriously, y'all should have seen those girls checking him out when the limo dropped him off at his dorm on my birthday. It looked like they were ready to rip his clothes off and jump on top of him."

"You know lawn mower guy is too into you," Jalisa said.

"Seriously, he actually puts up with your crap," Diamond joked.

"Hey, Kenisha! Kenisha, you know you wrong."

We stopped laughing and turned around seeing Li'l T hurrying up behind us. We all groaned at the same time. It never failed. Whenever we were going someplace, Li'l T was always around following right behind us.

"What are you doing out this late?" Diamond asked.

"Shouldn't your mommy be tucking you in by now?" Jalisa added.

"Y'all think y'all funny. You just lucky I got a sense of humor, and I know that y'all be checkin' a brotha out when he's not around."

"Oh, please," we all said, then laughed.

"So what's up with you, girl? You getting all scandalous," he said to me.

"What are you talking about little boy?" I asked.

"You know what I'm talking about, you and D," Li'l T said.

"What, who's D?" Diamond asked.

"I have no idea who he's talking about," I said. But I presumed he meant Darien. For once I would love it if Li'l T would keep his mouth shut.

"Oh, come on, girl, acting like you don't know. I saw you."

"Saw me what? What are you talking about?" I asked.

"You know you don't need to be hanging with D. That dude is wrong. He hangs with gang members, and they say he sells drugs."

"You don't even know him," I said, not believing him.

"Everybody knows D. He's got drama on his back like white on rice. Brotha is always in deep. See, I thought you and TB were hanging? Guess not."

"Who's D?" both Jalisa and Diamond asked.

"And who's TB?" Jalisa added.

"I thought you were hanging with lawn mower guy," Diamond said.

"What's a lawn mower guy?" Li'l T asked.

"Oh, please, you don't even know what you're talking about Li'l T."

"I know I saw you getting out his car the other day after you kissed him," he said.

Jalisa and Diamond looked at me with their mouths wide open. I glared at Li'l T. He was always up in somebody's business. Sometimes he just needs to keep his mouth shut.

"It's not what you think you saw, so don't even try it. He gave me a ride home after school. That's all. And for your information, I didn't kiss him, he kissed me. Now if you're gonna spread rumors, at least get it right." I turned and started walking. I was pissed, and I was seriously ready to slap him. I hate having all my business out in the street. I wasn't ready for my girls to know about Darien, but I guess I had to now thanks to big mouth Li'l T.

"Yo-yo-yo. Hey, Kenisha. I was only playing with you, girl," he said. "Come on, Kenisha. Kenisha!" He called out, but I just kept walking. Diamond and Jalisa started walking behind me.

"Girl, don't worry about Li'l T. You know he's just acting stupid like he always do," Jalisa said.

"Seriously, he just always need something to say. You know how he is," Diamond added.

They caught up with me as I slowed down. "Fine, we kissed. Terrence doesn't know 'cause he's never around anymore. Come on, let's go in." We stopped in front of Ursula's house. I climbed the front steps. The door was open, but I rang the doorbell anyway. Ursula's mom came

to the door. "Hey, come on in. Just go down the hall. Ursula and Darien are downstairs."

"Thanks and happy birthday," I said. We walked to the back of the house and went downstairs. The go-go music, Washington's twenty-year old homestyle sound, was loud and the place was already packed. There was actually an MC on the mic spinning the eclectic freestyle mix of hip-hop and funk. It was music we'd danced to for years, so we were already loving it. We walked along the packed dance area. It was dark, so I couldn't see much of anything, but I heard my name called. I turned. It was Ursula.

"Hey girl, I was wondering what happened to you," she said.

"I'm here. Wait, these are my girls," I said and turned as Jalisa and Diamond moved closer. "Jalisa and Diamond, this is Ursula."

They greeted each other and then this guy came up and asked Diamond to dance. It always happened like that. Diamond was too pretty. She had this China doll thing going on. As soon as she walked away, another guy came up and asked Jalisa to dance. When she left, Ursula and I started talking.

"Hey, you look good," someone said, behind me.

I turned knowing the voice. It was Darien. "Hi," I said smiling. Damn, he looked good too, but I didn't say that.

"You want something to drink," he asked.

"Nah, I'm okay," I answered. I make it a serious rule never to take a drink from anybody and never to walk away from my drink to dance. People are crazy out here. They spike drinks with date rape drugs, ecstasy, crack,

meth and just plain drugs, just to have fun. I don't think it's funny. So anyway, he asked me to dance.

We danced a few times then a slow song came on. Mostly everybody started pairing up, but I saw Diamond and Jalisa on the side talking to Ursula and two other girls I recognized from around the way. I started walking toward them when Darien held my hand and pulled me back. I bumped right into him. He put his arm around my waist and pulled me close. My heart was beating so fast I thought I was going to pass out. All of a sudden it got hot in there.

So we were slow dancing and he moved closer, trying to grind his body against mine. Okay, I dated LaVon, I know when a guy is trying to grind on me. "I'm all sweaty and hot, I gotta sit down," I said. That's always my standard back off line. I eased back.

"Come on, baby. Dance with me," he said, still holding my hand.

"We did just dance, but I'm just tired now, that's all. It's hot in here," I said, then started fanning my face with my fingers. The modest crowd had swelled to full capacity. I could barely move to get back to where my girls were standing.

"A'ight, then why don't you come outside with me?"

He was smiling, and I was smiling. I was tempted. "A'ight."

thirteen

Caution: Merging Drama Ahead

"The devil you know is much scarier than the devil you don't. But when you're surrounded and they all look alike, how do you tell which devil is which? Forget the pitchfork and horns thing. They don't do that anymore. Look closer."

—MySpace.com

We went toward the back door. My girls and I called ourselves getting to the party fashionably late, but people were still arriving as Darien and I were walking out. It was obvious the word was out that this was the place to be tonight. I looked back once seeing my girls talking and laughing, so I figured it was okay to go with Darien for awhile. After all, I was just stepping outside to get some fresh air.

He was holding my hand and guiding me through all these people lined along the walls. He'd say a few words to somebody, laugh at something somebody else said in his ear, or just shake hands or bump fists. But all the time we were walking, he never thought about introducing me to anyone. They all looked at me like they knew something. Wrong. They didn't know anything. Somebody handed him a can of beer. He took it then kept walking.

As soon as we hit the back door, the smell of stank, sweat, cigarettes and marijuana was thick. It was like cutting through a funk-fog. My stomach lurched, but I kept walking. There was a mild argument then scuffle behind me. I saw people looking back, but I didn't bother. I just, for real, needed fresh air now and kept on walking.

"Darien, Darien, wait."

He turned, I did too. Cassie was hurrying outside behind us. I smiled seeing her, but she just looked at me strange like I was totally out of place or something. "Hi, Cassie," I said.

"Oh, hey," she said to me then focused her attention on Darien. "Umm, Darien, I need to ask you something," she said.

"What?" he asked, with attitude.

"Umm, it's umm," she began then paused and looked at me. I knew she wanted me to leave, but I wasn't going anywhere. Besides, Darien was still holding on to my hand. "Umm, never mind. I'll ask you later."

He instantly turned and continued walking. I followed. "What was all that?"

"Who knows? Cassie's a joke," he said, dismissively.

"No she's not, she's nice. We walk home from school sometimes. I like her."

"Girl, you don't even know her," he affirmed.

I thought about what he said. He was right, I didn't really know her, but she seemed nice to me, so I guess that was okay. But then again, my ex-friend Chili seemed okay to me too, and look how all that turned out. Anyway, she was okay with me so, whatever. But I wondered why he would just come right out and diss her like that. "So don't you think you need to find out what she wants?" I asked.

"I know what she wants, and she's gonna have to wait."

I opened my mouth to ask what he was talking about but then changed my mind. So we finally moved away from everybody, got outside and started walking down the alley. I saw his car parked on the street just as the alley stopped. He held his keys, the car beeped and the headlights turned on. I stopped. "Hold up, wait," I said, stopping. He kept going but stopped when I shook my hand loose from his. "I'm not going for a ride with you."

"I thought you wanted some air," he said.

"Hello, this is air, Earth Science 101," I joked.

"Air conditioning," he said. "We're not driving anywhere. I just thought you wanted air conditioning to cool off."

All right, it was hot, even for the end of October, it was hot. "Fine, but I'm not going anywhere. My girls are still back at the house, and I'm not leaving them."

He opened the door and we got in. He turned on the engine then the air conditioner. Cool air streamed out of the small vents on the dashboard. He adjusted the center vents to blow directly on me. "Okay, trust me now?" he asked.

I did feel kind of silly. I just settled back and relaxed feeling the cool breeze on my damp body. It felt nice. I watched as he pulled a small vial out of his pocket. "What's that?" I asked. He tipped a small amount of white powder onto his baby finger then held it to one nostril and inhaled quickly. He tossed his head back and coughed then he closed his eyes sated. I watched in amazement. I'd never seen anyone get high before.

"You want some?" he asked, finally looking at me.

I shook my head. He had to be kidding. All the things I know about drugs, hell no. "Nah, I'm good," I said feeling nervous for some reason.

"Come on. Try it. It'll loosen you up," he cajoled.

"I'm loose enough," I said, watching as he repeated the action with his other nostril. I looked away. It was time to get out of there. "I'm ready to go back."

"Nah, come on. Hang with me." I heard the sound of a tab being pulled back. He opened the beer and offered me a sip. "Nah, I don't drink," I said, "I don't like the taste of it."

"You ever try it," he asked. I shook my head no. "Then how do you know if you don't like it?"

"I tasted champagne before. My mom used to drink Veuve Clicquot Ponsardin and Opus One all the time."

"Expensive. You didn't like them?"

"They were okay, I guess," I said, acting like I knew what I was talking about. Actually, I took one sip of Opus One and nearly gagged. I started choking and coughing. Afterward I swallowed almost a gallon of water to get the bitter, nasty taste out of my mouth.

"Here, try it," he offered.

"Nah, that's okay," I said.

"You're scared," he insisted.

"I'm not scared of anything." I grabbed his can of beer

and put it to my lips. I held my breath and took a sip then choked and spit it out. It was horrible, worse than the Opus One. I started wiping the beer off the front of me. My shirt was wet and stinking. But before I could say anything more, Darien was all on top of me kissing me. I moved back and pushed him off.

"Aw come on, let's not play this virgin game. You were swinging with TB and LaVon. I know those brothas. They handle their business."

"Yeah, but not with me," I said, then got out. I started walking down the alley back to the party. He caught up with me quickly.

"Kenisha, Kenisha, I'm sorry. Look I'm sorry. I was wrong. I heard that you were a good girl. I just wanted to make sure. There's all these posers out here trying to mess a brotha up."

"Whatever, Darien," I said. I kept walking, but I knew he was talking about Sierra. I got back to the party and headed straight for my girls. As soon as I saw them I was relieved. I was just about to join them, when this guy asked me to dance so I did. I knew Darien was back inside and that he was probably watching me, so I danced. I wanted him to know that his little show didn't bother me one bit—even though it did.

I was dancing and pushing all up on the guy having fun. He was trying to say something to me, but the music was too loud. I guess he must have smelled the beer 'cause he asked if I wanted another one. I just ignored him like I hadn't heard what he said. So I was dancing. Then I saw that Diamond, Jalisa and Ursula were dancing, too. We all started clowning and dancing like we do at Freeman. Ursula was right in there with us.

We were having so much fun playing around like that. After a while, some of the people stopped dancing and were just watching us. We were center stage freestyling. When the songs went off, we broke up laughing and everybody started clapping.

So it was getting late and the birthday party upstairs had long since broken up. It was now just the party in the basement and in the back alley. Ursula went upstairs in the refrigerator and got me, Jalisa and Diamond some bottled water. I told her that I never drink anything already open at parties. So we were standing around talking and drinking water. Darien came up to me.

"Girl, you were tight out there. Where'd you learn to do that?"

"Freeman dance class," I said, getting my breath back. Between the heat and the heavy dancing, we were all tired and breathing hard.

"That was…" Ursula started, still panting hard. We were probably in better breathing shape than she was. "That was fun."

"See, you need to get back to dance class," I told her.

"You used to go to Freeman?" Jalisa asked.

"That's where I saw you. I knew I recognized you from somewhere," Diamond added. "Girl, you were good out there."

"So you gonna introduce me to your girls or what?" Darien asked.

I looked at him like he was crazy. The whole time we

were going outside he never once introduced me to any of his friends—not that I was interested in meeting them anyway. But whatever, so I didn't have to say anything 'cause Ursula introduced everybody. After that Diamond and Jalisa were back dancing and it was just me Ursula and Darien standing there.

"Hey, Kenisha, I thought that was you."

I turned around. Leelah, some girl I met last month who went to school with Jade, was there. "Hey," I said, happy to see her. We talked a bit, and she asked about Jade and Tyrece and his tour. I told her that they were fine. Then we talked more, and she walked away.

"Whoa, whoa, whoa, check, you know Tyrece Grant?" he asked.

"More like he knows my sister," I clarified.

"Where you been D, under a rock?" Ursula joked. "Jade and Tyrece are getting married, and Jade is Kenisha's sister. Tyrece hung out at her sixteenth birthday party. I heard he did a concert for her and all his friends showed up. Chris Brown, Tyga and Lil'Wayne was there, too."

He turned and looked at me different but didn't say anything. I wish I knew exactly what he was thinking, or maybe not. "Come on, let's dance," he said to me.

"Nah, that's okay. I'm too tired now," I said sipping my bottle still. I saw Sierra. She must have come late. She was over against the wall hanging with the same girls she was hanging with when we first met, plus Cassie. Sierra was glaring at me. I had no idea why. I guess she thinks that I want Darien. To tell you the truth, I don't really know what I want. At least he's around.

The same guy that I was dancing with before asked me to dance again. I said sure and then looked at Darien as I followed the other guy to dance. I could tell he was pissed that I was dancing with somebody else, but I didn't care.

After a while I was just dancing and having fun with the guy and my girls. I forgot all about Darien and Sierra and their drama. We were just having fun.

Then there was some kind of commotion at the back door. Everybody went back to see what was going on, but nobody who was actually dancing stopped. We just looked around then went back to having fun. When a couple of people came back from checking it out, they told Ursula that it was Darien up to his old tricks fighting again. She looked at me and just rolled her eyes. I laughed. Whatever happening had to happen without us.

fourteen

2 Far Out of Bounds

"Testing the water is something we learn in child-hood. Don't just jump in. Test it first. It might be too hot or too cold. Well, to hell with all that. I'm jumping in head first, ya heard. Now, mess with that..."

—MySpace.com

After another three or four songs went off, a slow song came on. The dance area practically cleared out. The basement was starting to clear out anyway since it was already really late. We decided to head home. Ursula walked us upstairs and to the front door after getting us more bottles of water. She told us about a go-go party going on at this teen hangout in Charles County, but we weren't sure if we could go. I told her I'd call her later and let her know for sure.

We were starting to walk down the street when Darien drove up with one of his friends. He stopped beside us. "Hey, y'all ain't finished for the night, are you?"

We stopped. "Why, what you got?" I asked. I was

showing off for my girls since I could see Diamond and Jalisa look at each other.

"There's a dance battle going on at the hall," he said.

"A dance battle," Jalisa repeated, interested.

Diamond scrunched up her face. It was weird 'cause out of the three of us she was the best dancer, singer, best everything. I would have sworn she'd be jumping all over the invitation to go.

"Come on," Darien said, "it's just at the hall. I'm headed over there now."

It was cool with me. I grabbed the car handle instantly. I didn't even have to think about it twice. I was there. But then I looked back at my girls. Neither had moved. "Come on, y'all," I said. Diamond looked at Jalisa and then they looked at me. By now I was already seated in the car waiting. "Come on."

A few seconds later they got in the backseat with me. The car took off instantly. The music was loud, and a thin veil of marijuana hung in the air. His friend turned around several times trying to talk to Diamond, but there was no way she was interested in him. He was one hundred percent street, and that just wasn't her. Obviously getting nowhere with her, he shifted his conversation to Jalisa. That was a waste of time, too.

So we drove for like what seemed like an hour. We wound up on this dilapidated half road bumping on gravel and crossing some old railroad tracks. There were all these warehouses lined up, and I could see the D.C. skyline in the far, far distance.

"Where are we?" Jalisa whispered to me.

I shrugged. I had no idea. A few turns later we drove up to a dimly lit warehouse with all these cars parked out front. There was no order. It was like the driver just pulled up, stopped and jumped out. Anyway, we get out and walk up to this guy standing at the door. Darien said something to him and he just let us in.

As soon as the door opened, the music was blaring loud. Diamond said something, but I couldn't hear her and I was even walking right next to her. So we kept going, following Darien and his friend. We entered this massive open space, and right in the center, all these people were crowded around laughing and talking and dancing.

As we approached, a few guys saw Darien and pounded his fist or shook his hand. It was like we were with a celebrity. They were giving him mad props. It was like he ran the place or something. So walking in with him instantly gave us street cred.

Some of the people parted to let him through. I followed, then Diamond and Jalisa were after me and then the other guy, Darien's friend, was last. We walked right through the crowd and stood right up front. There were two dance crews about to battle. One crew was dressed in all black and the other had on jeans and no shirts. Jalisa hit my shoulder and I turned. Her jaw had dropped and the smile on her face was priceless.

So the three of us stood watching and waiting. Then the music started and the place went wild. The three dancers dressed in black started to battle. I never saw anything like it in my life. They were incredible. They did pop and lock and freestyle, then they clowned on the other crew. The crowd was yelling, screaming and laughing like crazy. Then, the other crew danced, and they went back and forth like that for the length of the music. My eyes were all over the place. It was like a clip from a movie, but this was for real.

These were real dancers and real crews, and real money was flying around. Every time a new crew stepped up to battle, money came out. People were making bets all over the place. Then this one crew stepped up, and people starting getting pissed about something. They started yelling and throwing things, so the crew stepped back. I have no idea what all that was about, but it was real scary. I thought they were going to fight up in there.

So anyway, these other two crews stepped up and the battle began. They were both, for real, good. Diamond, Jalisa and I were really feeling them. They could have been professional. I've seen dancers in movies and on stage who didn't look as good as they did. They even had a girl in the crew, and she was too tight.

After all the crews had a turn, they opened the dance floor to anyone who wanted to freestyle. We tried to get Diamond to get out there, but she wouldn't. Jalisa said no, so I got my butt out there and worked it. Yeah, that's right, I tore it up. I was doing all this stuff that I'd seen the girl on the crew do, and people were cheering me on. Then I was dancing with this guy, and they really went wild. I had a blast. After a while, everyone got out and started dancing, and that's when Diamond and Jalisa joined in. We outdid ourselves doing what we'd learned from Gayle and Jade.

An hour later, Darien dropped us off at my grandmother's house. It was almost dawn so we tried to be quiet going in, but my grandmother heard us anyway. She asked if we had a good time. I was surprised that she wasn't upset that we'd been out so late. But I don't officially have a curfew. So Diamond, Jalisa and I literally crashed in my bedroom and woke up late the next morning. Our ears where still buzzing from the loud music.

"What is that heavenly smell?" Diamond asked.

I looked at her puzzled then answered, "Breakfast."

"Girl, your grandmother is a saint. She makes you breakfast?"

"Only on the weekends," I said.

"You are so lucky, and I can't believe she was so cool about us coming home so late last night. My mom would have hit the roof," Diamond said.

"Tell me about it. I'd still be hearing the lecture," Jalisa added.

We went down for breakfast. The kitchen table was piled high with bacon, sausage and scrapple. We also had pancakes, eggs and melons. We said grace then dug in. We told my grandmother all about the party and how we took center stage dancing. Then Jalisa got up and started showing my grandmother one of the moves. We laughed so hard when my grandmother stood up next to her and started imitating her.

"Grandmom, you look good," I said.

"Go grandmom, go grandmom, go grandmom," Jalisa and Diamond chanted.

"All right, all right, that's enough of that," she said

catching her breath. "I'm gonna get some gardening done. You girls clean up the kitchen."

"Sure, then we have to get to Freeman, okay," I said.

"Fine, see you later," she said, then headed out the back door to her garden.

We cleaned up the kitchen and washed the dishes. When everything was done, we got our dance bags and headed to Freeman. We got there early so we sat around talking and stretching. Of course we talked about the party the night before. We all had a great time. "So y'all want to go to the go-go thing in Charles County tonight with Ursula?" I asked.

"I gotta babysit for Natalie tonight," Jalisa said.

"Nah, I'm supposed to go out with my mom," Diamond said.

"Okay, I'll tell her," I said.

"You know the party was tight and all. I liked it and had a good time after a while, but some of them girls were ready to kick our butts up in there," Jalisa said.

"Yeah, what was up with that? When you left for awhile I got into it with some girl, but Ursula stepped in," Diamond added.

"For real, why you didn't tell me this before? Who was it?"

Diamond shrugged. "I have no idea, but she came in pissed." I immediately thought of Sierra, but then Cassie came to mind, too. She was acting strange after Darien and I walked away. "It was like four of them up in my face. Ursula was upstairs with her mom, but came down just as she was getting all stupid."

"Where did your butt go, and why were you drinking?"

"Yeah, your breath was kicking, and you smelled like beer."

"What?" I said shocked. "I wasn't drinking last night." Then it hit me. I did take a sip of Darien's beer. They looked at me knowing better. "Yeah, okay, when I went out to get some air I went to Darien's car. He was drinking a beer. I took a sip, but it was horrible. I gagged and choked then spit it out. It dribbled down the front of my shirt."

"I thought we promised after we were playing around with your mom's Opus One that we wouldn't drink until we graduated college," Jalisa said. Diamond nodded.

"We did, and technically I didn't swallow. I spit it out. So I didn't actually drink." I knew I was fronting even as I was saying it. They were right. I broke a promise.

"And what was up with you dancing all suggestive like that? Are you crazy or something?"

"For real, girl, you looked like one of those hoochie-mommas on those triflin' rap videos."

"I did not," I said.

"Well, that guy who jumped up to freestyle with you seemed to think so. I'm just glad everyone else started dancing too 'cause dude looked like he was about to pounce."

"Don't even try it. I was just doing what that other girl on that crew did."

"And didn't you think she looked raunchy?"

"She was a'ight," I lied, knowing that she looked too nasty. We talked some more about the night before. Then class started a few minutes later. It was jazz tap. That meant constant movement. We left completely worn out. Our legs and muscles were done. We barely got back to my grandmother's house. Diamond and Jalisa gathered their overnight bags and loaded Diamond's car. "I'll see y'all later."

"Kenisha, be careful," Diamond said.

"Yeah, don't be posing like that," Jalisa added.

"See y'all," I said, then watched as they got in the car and drove off. I couldn't believe what they were talking about. I wasn't posing. This was me. This is how I've always been. I turned back to my grandmother's house.

"Hey, Kenisha."

I turned. "Hey, Cassie," I said.

"Were those your girls just now?"

"Yeah."

"You need to tell them to chill next time. Acting all uppity only gets them hurt."

"What do you mean?" I asked.

"I'm just saying," she said, not elaborating.

"Jealously is so ugly, Cassie."

"Ain't nobody jealous."

"Uh-huh," I said, seeing the green all over her face.

"Well, anyway, you going to the go-go tonight?"

"I don't think so," I said. I wasn't sure I could get out and party two nights in a row. Besides, I had church in the morning.

"You should come," Cassie said. "We always have fun, and Darien will probably be there."

I grimaced. "Why should that matter? I don't care what Darien does."

"I heard that y'all was hitting it. You went to his car last night, right?" she asked. I nodded. "And he hit it, right?"

"Hell, no," I almost shouted.

"Well, everybody thinks you did."

"Well, everyone is wrong," I said sternly. I started to see that Cassie was a troublemaker. She seemed to enjoy hating on people, but not like Li'l T. He told to inform and warn people of what he'd heard. Cassie seemed to like telling things to start trouble. "And you can tell Sierra I said so. I don't want Darien, period."

"Chill girl, you getting all serious on me, I was only telling you what's out there. And you know Sierra and I don't talk like that anymore."

"Whatever," I said. "I gotta go in and do some homework. See you later." I went to my room and just sat at the desk. I pulled out a few books, but I wasn't in the mood to do any homework. I hate when things like that happen. I didn't do anything, but now just because of the circumstances, it looked like I did. I didn't drink, but my girls thought I did. I didn't do anything with Darien, but now everybody thought I did. This was ridiculous. My cell rang. It was my dad at home, so I picked up.

We talked a minute then he asked me to go online. I did. There was a conference call message. I opened the program and turned on the camera. The first faces I saw were Jr. and Jason. I started laughing. "Hey Pineapple-head, hey Coconut-head," I said. They broke up laughing. Jason touched the screen like he expected to touch my face. "I'm in D.C. You guys being good?" I asked. They nodded still amazed at seeing and hearing me. "What are you guys doing now?"

Jr. started first. He told me about his new best friend and how they played yesterday, and then Jason joined in, telling me about his new toy. We talked a while. I was surprised how much I missed talking to them. They were like two cartoon characters that always made me laugh and feel good. I guess it was the fact that they were still kids and had no idea how hard things could get. "All right, Burt and Ernie. Put Dad back on."

"I'm Burt. Go get Dad, Ernie," Jr. insisted.

"No, I'm Burt, you're Ernie. You go get Dad," Jason said.

They started arguing and then pushing. "Stop it," I said loud enough to get their attention. "Stop it, don't be fighting. Both of you go get Dad. I'll wait. And for the record, you're both Burt and Ernie. Now go and walk. Don't run in the house." They called our dad as I watched them disappear from the screen. A few seconds later I saw my dad's face. He was smiling.

"What did you say to them just now?"

"Nothing, why?" I asked.

"They walked into the living room and told me you wanted to see me. I swear I've never seen them actually walk before."

"I just told them to stop running in the house, that's all."

He shook his head. "I told them that a million times and so has Courtney. I guess she was right. They do listen to you more than they listen to us." He smiled happily.

We talked more, mainly about school and Hazelhurst. Another exam was coming up at the end of the month, and he wanted to make sure I was going to be ready. I assured him that I'd be ready then signed off. I checked to see if Terrence sent me anything. He didn't. I did have a text message from Ursula asking if I was going tonight. I didn't know how to answer. I wanted to go, but I knew my grandmother would have a fit.

So as usual, Saturday evenings my grandmother cooks dinner. She was tired after gardening all day, so I volunteered to cook and clean up. When she went to bed early, I changed clothes, peeked in at her passed out and snuck out of the house. I met Ursula down the street and then Darien drove to the after-hours go-go party in Charles County.

I had no idea what to expect. But, for real, I didn't expect the go-go party to be in an old beat-up restaurant. "This is the go-go party?" I asked as Darien found a place to park not far from the entrance. A constant motorcade of minivans and mom cars flowed by discharging teen-agers. Doors slid open and teens poured out. It was like a school drop-off point.

"By day it's a rib joint, but at night the owner hires it out to club promoters," Darien said.

"We used to go to this place a few miles from here, but they closed it down after somebody was shot and killed. Then there was this other place in D.C. we used to hang, but two stabbings and a gun fight later that was closed, too. There's this other place in Charles County, but the police get too controlling. So this is the spot now," Ursula said, cavalicrly.

I shivered. We got out and started walking toward the makeshift dance club. "So what's up with all the cops?" I asked, starting to get nervous inside. This was all new to me, but I was posing like I knew what to expect. For real, I had no idea.

"They bring drug-sniffing dogs and just stand around trying to harass people who just want to party instead of doing what the tax payers actually pay them to do," she said, talking louder and louder. Several of the police officers turned to glance at her. She eyed them, then sucked her teeth and rolled her eyes. I looked at her like she was crazy. Taunting cops wasn't exactly a natural occurrence for me.

So we got to the entrance. It was brightly lit like daytime. There were a few people in front of us. One was this huge mountainous guy and his friends. He laughed at something then lumbered to the side and leaned on the wall. It felt like the whole building shook. When he moved in, there was security in the foyer area. One guy was patting down the big dude, and another was waving a metal detector over the front of this girl's body. It beeped and everybody turned around, but it was just her belt buckle.

This other security guy told me to take off my boots. I looked at him like he was crazy. Why in the world did I need to take off my boots? Then Ursula tapped me on the arm and pointed to a wooden bench. We both sat down and removed our boots, and Darien leaned on the side wall and removed his sneakers. He slapped them together a couple of times then the security guy peeked inside and nodded. I offered one guy my boots, but he just motioned for me to tap the heels together. I did, and he nodded and motioned for me to go inside. This better be worth it, is all I'm saying.

I didn't know what the restaurant looked like during the day, but I put money on the fact that it didn't look like this. The lights were dim, and there were twirling, flashing lights mounted on the ceiling. There was a band at one end and people were dancing everywhere. Of course the place was packed.

"Come on, let's dance," Ursula said, pulling me along behind her. We got to a place near the center of the room and started dancing. Everybody just danced in the crowd; there was no pairing up. It was just fun. The music played nonstop for about an hour. We danced the whole time. They changed bands, and we danced some more.

So we're dancing and I heard my name. Li'l T was dancing near us. He waved. I nodded then shook my head to him. I wasn't exactly still mad at him, just maybe a bit annoyed. "Where your girls?" he asked when he danced closer.

"Home," I said, and then waited for some smart-alecky remark. It didn't come. He nodded without asking more. It was strange. Li'l T never shut up. He always had something to say. Then I saw him look over my shoulder, then look away. I glanced to the side. Darien was there. I figured that they must have some history that I didn't know about.

So we were having fun. The music was tight, and the dance floor was packed. After another half hour, we took a break and got something to drink. They were selling soda and water at the bar. We each got something then Ursula walked away to talk to some guy she knew, and I stood talking to Darien. We talked about the different go-go bands, the crowd, then the party the night before.

"So what's up with you and TB?" he asked, moving close so I could hear him better.

"What do you mean?" I asked.

"Y'all hanging out or what? I mean, I don't see him around, ever."

"Just 'cause you don't see him around doesn't mean he's not. I talk to him all the time. He's busy that's all."

He looked me up and down then shook his head. "If I was hitting this, I'd been here twenty-four, seven."

"Well, I don't see you with Sierra."

"That's 'cause we ain't together."

"That's not what I hear, *Daddy*," I said smiling knowingly.

He smiled too then nodded. "Yeah, yeah, that's right. But it ain't about all that now. I made a mistake. We both did. We're dealing but it, but it doesn't mean we have to be together, right?" he asked. I shrugged. He had a point.

"So TB, huh?" he said.

"Terrence," I corrected. "So what's up with you and Terrence? You know him. Why all the hostility?"

"He ain't tell you?" he asked.

"Tell me what?" I asked.

"Nah, nah, never mind. So what do you see in him?"

"He's nice, he's smart and he's fun to be with."

"Sounds more like a punk-ass chihuahua to me," he said dismissively.

"Oh, and he doesn't dog me. He treats me right."

"Is that all it takes to get with you?" he asked.

"It helps. Terrence is a good guy."

"Oh so what, you trying to say I'm not?" he asked.

"I'm saying that you come with drama. Sierra for instance…"

"I told you, ain't nothing to all that," he interrupted.

"…yeah, I know. But it's not just about all that. You're dangerous. You got bad boy written all over you."

"And you don't hang with bad boys."

I shrugged. "You're the type that girls hang with for awhile, but…"

"But you can't take me home to meet your grandmom."

"You'd be staking the place, and you know it," I said.

He laughed. "See, it ain't even about all that. I don't rob people. That's kid stuff. And as for hanging with bad boys, you need to check yourself. TB ain't no saint either."

"Yeah, but that was then. This is the for real stuff now."

"So you saying I can't change?" he asked.

"Sure you can. And after house arrest, maybe you should."

"Check, your man's a poser. He acts like he's all down. He's doing all that college stuff, walking around like he better then somebody else. But for real, he ain't all that."

"What's wrong with going to college and wanting a better life?" I asked.

"It ain't about all that. He just needs to be for real."

I didn't get what he was saying, but before I could find out more, one of his boys came over and said something to him in his ear. He nodded, told me he had to leave and then followed the other guy through the crowd. I was getting hot and tired, plus I was curious, so I followed him. He went outside and walked around to the side of the building.

So Darien and his friend walked over to these guys who were standing all together laughing, smoking and talking. I could see a few cops were hovering by, so I didn't get too close. Darien and his friend walked up and everybody greeted everybody else. Then there was some kind of big scuffle on the other side of the parking lot 'cause the cops took off running in that direction. Everybody turned to see what was happening, but they didn't move.

I looked back to the front of the building seeing that the crowd outside was getting thicker. It was like everybody knew something was about to go down and they wanted to be there, either to witness it, get involved in it or to get away from it.

A few more guys walked over to where Darien stood. I moved closer, curious. By now I could smell the stench of marijuana in the air. I stood with these other girls just a few feet away from another commotion. Sierra was there too. We looked at each other but didn't speak. I was just turning to go back inside when I heard popping sounds. Everybody knew what that meant.

fifteen

Fast & Furious

"Whoa, so when did out of control become the norm? For real, I can see myself free-falling without a parachute holding a lead ball in each hand. No stopping, no pausing, just fast and furious falling into whatever comes next."

—MySpace.com

somebody screamed, and then all at once everybody either ducked down or started running. I ducked down beside a parked car and stayed there. I watched the scene around me like it was happening to somebody else. It was crazy chaotic. People were running, screaming, yelling, pushing. I'd heard about stuff like this happening, but I never in million years thought I'd be in the middle of it. The girl ducking down next to me pulled out a cell and called somebody. She started relaying what was happening around us like a war correspondent.

It seemed to me that she thought this was no big deal, like it was a joke. She was bragging instead of being scared.

I couldn't believe it. She was actually joking about what was happening. Whatever I guess, bump this, I just stayed low. My heart was pounding a mile a minute, and my chest tightened. I took a deep breath, but it seemed that my lungs weren't filling up. I have asthma sometimes, mostly when I get stressed. I was obviously stressed.

I reached into my pocketbook to get the inhaler I always keep with me. I opened my mouth and pressed the button then inhaled deeply. I felt a quick cool blast stream down my throat and into my lungs. I sat back and waited. After a while I could breathe a little better. Still keeping low, I peeked up, looked around and then slowly stood. Most of the craziness was over, but all of a sudden a swarm of teens appeared out of nowhere, I guess mostly from inside the club.

They were just standing around laughing, talking, pushing, shoving or just walking around aimless, like they were waiting for something else to happen. Some were even standing on top of cars. I was close to a few shoving fights, but nothing came of it. I started walking, looking around for Ursula and Darien. I had enough of this. The police were everywhere, and I heard more sirens coming. I turned around and saw a cop use a Taser on this guy and then reach for his nightstick. Yeah, it was seriously time to go now.

As I moved through the crowd, rumors were flying as somebody asked somebody else what had happened. *"Somebody got shot. The back of the building was on fire. Two gangs were fighting. There was a drive-by shooting. Somebody stabbed somebody, and the cops are searching people for knives. A drug dealer executed somebody out back. Destiny's Child was back together and had shown up to party. Firecrackers were set off. The place had been robbed."* I couldn't believe all the wild stories. There was no telling what was real or not.

I kept looking around. It seemed now everybody was on a cell phone talking about what was happening. Then I saw this girl on the ground. She was searching around and yelling about finding her other earring. I couldn't believe she was actually worried about an earring. Then, for some reason, I still don't know why, everybody started running again. They were headed right in her direction. At the last minute, she jumped up and out of the way just before being trampled. It was crazy.

I kept looking for Ursula. After a while I saw Sierra again. We were right next to each other. There was a loud popping sound again and everyone ducked down, including me. I looked up, Sierra was still standing. I reached up and grabbed her hand and pulled her down beside me. She looked at me. She looked like she'd seen a ghost. "Stay down," I ordered.

The cops were running toward the popping sounds. "Come on," I said, still holding on to her hand, "let's get back inside the restaurant." We stood up, crocked low, then ducked behind some parked cars until we got to the side of the building. Just as we were making our way to the front door again, we saw Darien.

He and this other guy were fighting. I recognized that it was the same guy who found him before when we were inside the club talking. Sierra and I were moving closer when we saw the fight expand and others start jumping in. Now it was just a mess. They were all pushing, shoving and arguing.

The guy punched Darien hard. He fell to the side and hit against the side of the building. Darien charged him, and they both fell down. Then Darien got up first and kicked the other guy still on the ground. Somebody bumped into Darien, and the guy on the ground got up fast. He punched Darien again. Then I saw Darien pull something from behind his back. He held it out, and everybody stepped back.

Seconds later the police arrived. The fight broke up instantly and everybody scattered. The police were thick, but people were moving too fast. They caught a few guys but that's it. The guy Darien was fighting had fallen and was trying to get up when the police got him. More police came trying to grab anybody they could get. I couldn't believe what I was seeing.

Darien got away and ran right toward us. He was looking all crazy scared. "Here, take this," he said to Sierra shoving something at her. She took whatever it was and we ran to the front door. It was locked, but a lot of people were out front so we just stayed with them. I looked around. Darien was gone.

After a while the restaurant security opened the doors and everybody inside spilled out. It was chaos all over again. Everybody was everywhere all screaming, yelling and talking at once. Cars started driving and horns were blowing. Pick-up rides began driving up and then the place got even worse.

The police were trying to get the traffic in order as

more police cars arrived. Two ambulances and a fire truck pulled around the side of the building. Then somebody said that the police were gathering witnesses to the stabbing.

I finally found Ursula. She had been in the club and had no idea what had happened. We started walking toward where Darien had parked the car. When we got there, the car was gone. I looked at Ursula as Sierra looked at me. We didn't know what to do next. She called Darien on her cell while we moved to the side and waited.

The place was like something out of a movie. People were running, shouting and there were police cars everywhere. "He's not answering," Ursula said. "Let's go back to the restaurant."

"We probably can't get back in the club," I told her.

Ursula sighed heavily and shook her head. "I don't know what else to do. It's way too far to walk."

"Is there a bus or a train or something?" I asked.

Ursula shrugged. "I have no idea. I don't know Charles County."

"Maybe we can find somebody to give us a ride home," I said. We started looking around to find somebody we knew. Ursula tried to call Darien again but still got no answer. "The police are starting to pull people again. Come on, let's walk down to the corner." We'd just turned to walk away when I heard somebody call my name. I turned but didn't see anybody so we kept going.

"Yo, yo, yo, Kenisha over here! Come on, get in. Hurry up!"

I was never so glad to see Li'l T in my life. The three of

us ran to the car he was hanging out of and got in. It was the size of a shoebox, but it didn't matter. We all crowded in and the driver took off just as more police cars were coming.

It was Li'l T's cousin's car—or rather his mother's car. She didn't know he had it since they both snuck out to go to the club. Big T, Li'l T's cousin, had just gotten his license, and they were celebrating. Big T took off as soon as we crowded in. Unfortunately, Big T had no idea where he was going. We got lost three times trying to get back to the city, but as long as we weren't back at the go-go club I didn't care.

When we finally got to D.C., Big T dropped us off at my house. He offered to take Ursula and Sierra home too, but they wanted to get out with me. I was so happy to be someplace safe that I kissed Li'l T on the cheek. Much to his surprise, so did Ursula and Sierra. Right before they drove off I heard him telling Big T that we were "Li'l T's Angels" and that's how he rolled 'cause he got it like that. I couldn't help but shake my head. That boy was too much. But tonight I really didn't care.

So Ursula, Sierra and I stood out front a few minutes before Ursula asked the obvious question. "So what the hell happened? I'm dancing and having fun then all of a sudden I heard that Destiny's Child was outside. Then I heard that somebody got shot." Sierra and I just looked at each other.

"You know, I am so sick and tired of going out to have fun, then have some fool mess it up for everybody. Why can't they just keep their drama-asses at home? Always starting trouble and getting people caught up in that mess," she continued. "Y'all know what happened. And where the hell is Darien?"

We looked at each other again. "He left," I said.

"Yeah, Kenisha, duh. I got that part. Where'd he go?" She dialed his cell again but didn't get an answer. "I can't believe he's still not answering. This is so wrong."

"Maybe his cell is just turned off."

"Wait, it wasn't him who got shot, was it?" she asked cautiously looking at both of us.

"No, we saw him after everything happened. He was fine," I said, just as a police car sped through the traffic light at the corner.

"So where is he, and why the hell did he leave us there?"

"I guess he had to leave. The police were grabbing up everybody, so maybe I guess with him just getting off house arrest he didn't want to get in trouble again."

"Whatever, it's still wrong. You don't just run off and leave people like that, especially your family. I told you he was selfish like that," she said.

I had to agree with her. His stuff was wrong. But if I saw what I think I saw, then I know why he did what he did. He was holding something in his hand when the fight ended. Then that guy fell. If I didn't know any better, I'd swear that the guy he was fighting got stabbed.

Sierra hadn't said a word the whole time. She just looked from me to Ursula as we talked. We heard another police car siren somewhere in the neighborhood then saw it careen against the light and down the street. "I gotta go," Sierra finally spoke.

"Yeah, me too, let's go. Talk to you later, Kenisha," Ursula said as she and Sierra walked away. Sierra looked back at me but still didn't say anything to me.

I heard Ursula complaining again about fools messing up her good time. I waited a minute. Then after they got to the end of the block I went up on the porch and looked down the street and waited. I couldn't exactly see Ursula's house from my house, and the only window with a good enough view that faced in the right direction was in my grandmother's bedroom. Hopefully she was still asleep, which is where I should be. But I knew I was too hyped up to fall asleep anytime soon.

I sat down on the top step of the porch and just waited. I had no idea for what. I guess I just needed to take a break from everything that was going on and maybe try to wrap my head around it. My thoughts were spinning 'cause everything was happening so fast. I could barely hold on. All of a sudden my chest felt tight and breathing became difficult.

I reached into my purse and grabbed my inhaler but I didn't really need it, so I just sat there thinking about what had happened. After a while I found myself wondering about Darien and what had happened to him. I heard a siren again. It got louder as I saw a police car turn the corner away from my street. While I was looking down the street, I saw somebody walking up. I didn't want to be here when they got close, so I figured that it was time to go in. I stood and headed to the front door. "Kenisha."

I jumped and spun around.

"Chill girl, it's me," Darien said, as he walked up the

brick path to the front porch steps. He stopped at the bottom step and looked up at me. "Hey."

"Darien," I whispered, looking around cautiously. The last thing I needed is for my grandmother to wake up or for somebody else to see me with him. "Are you all right?"

"I'm always a'ight." He shrugged indifferently.

"So what are you doing here?" I asked.

"Hanging out, waiting," he said casually, like it was twelve noon instead of two-thirty in the morning.

"Waiting for what? You know you can't be out here in front of my grandmother's house late like this," I insisted.

"So why don't you invite me inside?"

"Hell, no," I said instantly.

"What, you don't want nobody to know that you into me?"

"Who said that I'm into you?" I asked, trying not to smile but failing miserably. I knew he could tell I was lying. The truth was I was kind of into him.

"Don't be frontin'. You know you like that bad boy thing you was talking about before. So why don't we just go inside and kick it?"

"Uh-uh. Plus it's late and I gotta go in."

"A'ight, fine. I just wanted to talk is all."

"Talk about what?" I asked, as I walked back to the top of the steps and sat back down.

Darien climbed the porch steps then sat next to me. He waited a few minutes, looked up and down the street then up at the sky. He pulled a cigarette and lit it. After a few deep drags, he looked at me. "You have a good time tonight?"

"I saw the fight," I said.

"Yeah, I figured that," he said.

"What were you fighting about?"

"Some punk-ass owes me money. Then he was gonna try frontin' like he don't know no better. I had to step up on him."

"Maybe he didn't have it on him at the time," I suggested.

"That's bull. He better step correct when he's handling my money and my business. He knows that now."

He took another hard drag of his cigarette then flicked it into the air. I watched the lit butt fall onto the brick path. I could tell he was still angry about the fight. His vernacular was all street and raw. Usually when he talked around me, he was different.

"So that guy works *with* you?" I asked, still watching the soft flame from the butt flicker.

"He works *for* me," he spat out the correction.

I wasn't sure I wanted to know anymore. He must have understood since he didn't volunteer anymore information. "So what's up?" I asked quietly. "Where did you go after that? We were looking for you. The police were everywhere. We barely got a ride home."

"I had to leave—too many cops. I don't want to go back to juvie hall."

"Then don't," I said, actually thinking it was that simple.

He half laughed at my naïveté. "You really think it's that easy, don't you? You think all I have to do is just not go."

"Isn't it?"

"No, it's not. This ain't some made for Disney movie, girl. This is real life."

"Like I don't know that? What I'm saying is that we all have choices in how and where we want to end up. Maybe you need to make another choice 'cause maybe the one you've made is gonna lead you back to where you don't want to be."

"You mean go back to school and all that crap."

"Yeah, why not? What's so bad about going to school? At least you have a chance for a better life and a future."

He chuckled again. "You really believe that, don't you?"

"I know that."

"See, it's that stuck-up bourgie private school that teaches you that shit. They brainwash you that all this can be better."

"Didn't I hear you went to private school, too?"

"Yeah, so what? Besides, that's different."

"How's it different?"

He looked at me then shook his head like he knew this big secret that I didn't. "You got this warped idea that life is any better than right now. It's not. I hustle, that's what life is. My dad's constantly on my case to go back to school or get my GED. He's pissed 'cause stuff be happening. He wants me to go work with him, but I can't be about all that. That nine-to-five ain't me, and that going to college shit sure 'nuff ain't me."

"So what do you think you're gonna do, just sit around and do nothing the rest of your life?"

"Nah, I got plans. I can produce videos and rap. I can be like Diddy."

"Doesn't everybody want to be like Diddy and think they can rap? So what are the odds of you actually having a career in the music business?"

"My pops could help me out, but he acting like he won't."

"Maybe he *is* trying to help you out."

"You know Tyrece Grant. Hook a brotha up," he said. I didn't respond. "See, you wrong and that's some bull," he said, louder than necessary. "See, you be talking to TB like that. That shit don't fly with me. I got a rep to protect."

"Your reputation, that's why you were fighting tonight?"

"Don't nobody disrespect me. I handle my business."

"You act like you do whatever you do because you have no choice, but you do—we all do. The bad boy thing won't last forever. Then what?"

"Then I'll get a new hustle, 'cause that's what you like about me and you know it."

I was just about to say something when he leaned over and kissed me. I was too shocked to do anything but just sit there. It's not like I never kissed anybody before, I have. But I was always kind of expecting it. Darien took me completely by surprise.

So he was kissing me, and I kind of kissed him back. We did that for a while. Then he leaned closer and started touching me. I let him then after a while I backed off. It felt funny. Yeah, I liked him and all, but I like lawn mower guy, too. Terrence was safe. Darien wasn't. I think he was right. I liked that he had a reputation and that he was a bad boy. We started kissing again. He took my hand and put it on his thigh. He moved it higher, and I felt him hard and jumped back.

"What, don't tell me you never been with TB before?" he said. "I know he's got your number punched." I didn't respond. He looked at me and shook his head. He obviously knew his answer. "Girl, he be playin' you. I hear brother be all over the place at Howard. He's got hunnies dropping at his feet morning, noon and night. Girl, you been played."

"I gotta go in," I said. This was getting way too real for me. I wasn't ready before with LaVon, and I know I was not ready now. I stood up, but Darien took my hand and held tight.

"Come on, stay," he said. "We don't have to do anything."

"I got church in a few hours, and after tonight, I need to get some sleep," I said easing my hand from his.

"A'ight, next time," he promised, "for real."

"Night," I said then headed to the front door. I unlocked it, went inside then locked it again. I didn't stop moving until I got to my bedroom. I was still shaking inside when I looked around my room. It was just like I left it, but somehow it seemed different. Maybe I seemed different.

I changed my clothes and lay in bed with my eyes open. Every noise made me jump. I still couldn't believe everything that went on that night. It was too wild. I never experienced anything like that before. It was crazy, everybody running around like that and the police all over the place. I couldn't wait to tell my girls about it. Then there was Darien. My stomach was still fluttering and my heart was going wild.

So by the time I finally dozed off, my alarm went off and it was time to get up. Sunday morning, I woke up feeling like somebody else. I wasn't me anymore. Last night was like a dream. No, make that a nightmare. I remembered being in Big T's car, closing my eyes all the way home, praying that we'd get there safe. I don't know what I was thinking sneaking out like that. I vowed never, ever, ever to do anything like that again. And I meant it.

So I went to church with my grandmother, and I could barely stay awake. After morning service we came home and had breakfast. We talked about school and other stuff while we ate. "So why are you so sleepy today?" she asked.

"I don't know. I didn't sleep well, I guess. I think I'm gonna go upstairs and crash now."

"Yes, you do that. You need to get your rest. Remember, I'm going back to church this afternoon. I'll bring something in for dinner."

I went upstairs and crashed. I must have slept for four hours. When I woke up, my grandmother was still out. I grabbed the newspaper and was checking out the metro section. There was an article in there about what happened last night at the go-go club. It mentioned that someone had gotten stabbed and was still in the hospital. The police were asking for witnesses to step up. Please, like that was actually going to happen.

Ursula called me and we talked a few minutes, mainly about the go-go club. She said that Darien had finally gotten home about four o'clock and that he was fine. She was still pissed that he left us there. She was just about to go off on a rant when my other line beeped. I told her that it was probably my dad so she hung up. I clicked over. It wasn't my dad. It was Terrence.

"Hey Shorty," he said happily.

"I thought you were supposed to be coming home this weekend," I said quickly.

"I thought so too, but I crossed over. We didn't know about it, it was a surprise. The whole line crossed. I'm officially a Greek."

He seemed so happy, but I wasn't feeling it. He promised that he'd be around, but he wasn't. At least Darien was here and acted like he wanted to be with me. "Congratulations," I said, not as delighted as I guess I could have been. He caught the bland tone in my voice.

"So what's up with you?"

"Nothing," I said, vaguely.

"You sound mad because I wasn't there this weekend?"

"Nah, I had fun. I hung out at my friend's house."

"What friends?"

"Ursula and Darien."

"Darien? What? You're hanging with Darien now?"

"He said y'all knew each other, but he wouldn't tell me how. You want to enlighten me?" I asked.

"You need to leave him alone," he warned sternly.

See that's something that pisses me off with Terrence. He thinks he can boss me around and tell me what to do. He can't. He says that we're hanging, but he's never around to hang with me. Maybe Darien was right. Maybe he was just playing me. "Why not? He's fun and at least he's around sometimes."

"You need to leave him alone," he repeated.

"Since when do you tell me what I need to do?" I asked. I was already irritated. His attitude was just getting me more annoyed. "So what's the beef between you two?

What, did he steal your toy in kindergarten or something?" I joked.

"I don't want to talk about it, but you need to listen to me and leave him alone."

"That's not good enough, Terrence."

"We'll talk about it Friday when I come by."

"Yeah, right. I heard that before." I half chuckled.

"What is wrong with you? You're acting all pissed off. I told you the line went over this weekend. I thought you'd be happy for me," he said. I didn't respond. "Kenisha. Kenisha?"

"I gotta go. I'll see you around, maybe." I hung up. I seriously don't know why I was so pissed off, but I was.

I decided to call Diamond and Jalisa. I needed to talk to someone real. We did our usual three-way conversation. We caught up on some homework business, and they e-mailed my assignments. We talked a little bit about school and Hazelhurst. But after that, the next thing out of Jalisa's mouth was that she saw the go-go club on the news this afternoon.

"Girl, I couldn't believe it. That's where Ursula was talking about going before, right?"

"I think so," Diamond said. "I wonder if she went."

"She went. We both did," I said casually.

"What?" Jalisa and Diamond said in unison.

"You went there last night?" Jalisa asked.

"No way. Your grandmother would never let you go out like that with church the next day," Diamond added.

"She didn't, but I did anyway. I snuck out."

"Kenisha," Jalisa, said, stunned, "you snuck out?"

"Yeah, my grandmother went to sleep early, so I left."

"Wait, so you were there when all the stuff on the news was going on?"

"Uh-huh. I even saw the guy who got stabbed."

"No, you didn't," Diamond said chuckling. "She's joking."

"I'm not joking. I saw it, for real."

"Kenisha, For real, for real?" Jalisa asked.

"Yep, for real," I said proudly.

"Girl what is up with you? You are moving too fast lately. First you going to parties where they're drinking and smoking pot. Then you're hanging out with this street thug drinking beer. Now you're sneaking out of the house and whatever else. You wrong and you know it," Jalisa said.

"For real, Kenisha," Diamond chimed in, "how can you just do that? Your mom would be so pissed if she was around."

"But she's not, is she?" I snapped. Suddenly I realized that this was going nowhere. My girls, my used-to-be girls, just didn't get it anymore. "She's gone, so I can do what I want."

"No, you can't," Diamond said.

"Whatever," I said dismissively.

"What is wrong with you?" Jalisa said.

"Nothing's wrong with me. What's up with you? Y'all acting all stuck up like you don't know how to have fun anymore. All you two do is hang out in the mall and shop. Please, living in the burbs got y'all all bourgie. Y'all don't know anything 'bout what goes on in the 'hood."

"In the 'hood," Diamond repeated with a chuckle.

"Like you do?" Jalisa snapped back. "Girl, please. Your butt grew up right down the street from us in the burbs, so don't be frontin' acting like you from the 'hood. And I don't know who you're calling, bourgie. You're the queen of bourgie."

"Don't even try it," I said, starting to get angry.

"Y'all need to chill on this and talk about something else. Who's going to dance this week?" Diamond said, attempting to change the conversation.

"Hanging around people who stab other people isn't exactly what I call fun," Jalisa continued. "And you don't either, remember? At least you didn't."

"You know what, I thought you guys would understand. I guess I was wrong," I said.

"Understand what?" Diamond asked.

"Understand that my life is different now. Things can't be the same as they were before. I live here. I go to school here."

"So what? You don't want to be friends with us anymore 'cause of where we live, is that what you're saying?" Jalisa asked cautiously. It got quiet.

"I didn't say that," I said quickly, as I felt my heart lurch. "It's just that everything is different."

"We're not different, Kenisha," Diamond said. "We're exactly the same as we always were."

"And you're not either. You just think you are 'cause you're mad. You're moving too fast, Kenisha. You need to slow down and chill."

"I'm not mad," I said calmly.

"Yeah, you are. You've been mad for awhile," Diamond said.

"It's true," Jalisa added.

"I'm not mad," I reiterated. "I'm fine. I just don't see why everybody's acting all different. Nobody understands anymore."

"Maybe you should talk to that guy again," Diamond offered.

"What guy?"

"That guy from school. The doctor, the shrink."

"Dr. Tubbs? What, you think I'm crazy now?" I asked.

"No, nobody's saying that. I think..." Jalisa started, then stopped.

"...We think you've been mad and pissed off for awhile. Maybe that's why you've been fighting. Maybe you need to talk to somebody about how not to be mad anymore."

"What if something happens, like you get in real trouble?"

"Nothing's gonna happen," I said, "Y'all are trippin'."

"We're just worried about you."

"Yeah," Diamond added.

"I'm fine. I gotta go, I have homework to do. I'll talk to y'all later," I said quickly, then hung up. This was getting stupid. I had no idea what was up with everybody. So what if I snuck out? So what if I hung out at a club when somebody got stabbed? It's no big deal. So what?

sixteen

No Exit

"I stood in a dark place, scared, alone, devoid of
form and feeling, devoid of light and laughter, devoid
of love. If I call out will anyone hear me? I don't
know anymore."

—MySpace.com

monday morning I staggered out of bed and went
to school. Of course everybody was talking about what
happened at Ursula's party Friday night and also about
the go-go club Saturday night. Everybody who wasn't
there wanted to know what happened, and everybody
who was there became an instant celebrity. I was at both,
so that made me the shit.

I wasn't in a great mood, but I dealt with it. After
school, I stayed for the extra class I was taking in English
lit. We'd already finished reading two books and were
now working on a poetry section. I was assigned to read
and analyze "The Negro Speaks of Rivers" by Langston
Hughes. I had to write an essay. I read the poem a few

times. I wasn't impressed. Then, when I read it a third time, I understood. He wasn't talking about rivers. He was talking about freedom. I started thinking about the idea of rivers being a simile for life and freedom. It made sense.

I wrote my essay the next day with that in mind. I equated it to feeling the loss of my mother and feeling misplaced by everything around me. It was probably some of my best work. I left school feeling great, but it was also weird. There was nobody to tell. I wanted to tell my girls about the essay, but I still hadn't spoken with either Diamond or Jalisa. It had been two days. We usually talk at least twice a day. The week was just about half over and neither of us called the other. I still don't get what they were talking about. I hadn't changed, not really. I was the same person I was before.

I don't know. But they were still my girls, even if they didn't get it. Then there was lawn mower guy, but I didn't need to think about him until the weekend, maybe. That is if he actually decided to show up. I still wanted to know what the drama was between him and Darien.

I walked home from school late Tuesday afternoon thinking about everything I had to do for the weekend. There was a party I was invited to, but I decided not to go. My Hazelhurst exam was over, but I still needed to stay on top of my studies. I was making a mental list when I heard my name called. I turned around.

"Kenisha, Kenisha. Girl, you hear me calling you."

Li'l T was standing there like he didn't recognize me. He probably didn't. Lately, I guess, I didn't recognize me either.

"What's up with you, Kenisha? You been weird all week."

"I've been busy," I said disinterestedly, then turned to start walking again. He walked beside me. We talked about school and then about the thing over the weekend.

"So, I saw your girls at Freeman yesterday. They looked pretty good. What happened to you? Why weren't you there?"

"Busy. Remember? I just told you," I snapped. The fact that Diamond and Jalisa went to Freeman Monday without telling me kind of hurt and made me mad. I don't know what they thought they were doing. I knew they had been talking about me behind my back.

"Yeah, I get your busy. So what are you gonna be?"

"What?" I asked getting annoyed for some reason. Li'l T was okay and all, but sometimes he was like a mosquito, always buzzing around and being annoying. "You mean career-wise?"

"Nah, for Halloween on Friday."

Great, that's the last thing I was thinking about, running around in a costume taking candy from strangers. "I think I'm a little old to be trick-or-treating."

"Aw, come on, it's fun. You remember fun, right?" he asked. I didn't say anything. I was remembering. "You know, I think you better chill on hanging with D. He 'bout to get you all tricked out, too."

"What makes you think I'm hanging with Darien?" I asked.

He looked at me and then just shook his head. "Dude gonna get you all messed up if you're not careful."

"I'm not messed up. I'm fine," I stated firmly.

"Sure you are. You acting just like him, all angry and pissed off at everybody for no reason, just like Sierra."

"What do you mean, just like Sierra?"

"And we won't even mention Cassie," he added.

"Cassie, what about Cassie?"

"Forget it, never mind," he said still walking. "You're probably too far gone into him anyway."

"No, tell me, what about Cassie. Were they together or something?" I asked catching up to him.

"Yeah, you can say that." He smirked sarcastically.

"Come on, tell me. I want to know."

"Kenisha," Darien called out from across the street. He was leaning against his car. I didn't even see him there.

Li'l T looked at me and then looked across the street, then back at me. He shook his head. "Later," he said, then walked away.

"Yeah, later," I said, standing there seeing him leave. I didn't get it. What was the big deal? It seemed that everybody was always hating on Darien. Jalisa, Diamond, Terrence, Ursula, Sierra, Li'l T and even my grandmother was acting like she was hating on him. I didn't get it. As far as I could see he was fine.

"Kenisha," Darien called out impatiently.

I walked across the street. "Hey, what's up?" I said.

"Come on. I'll give you a ride home."

"A'ight," I said, and then I got in the car. He didn't say anything more, he just drove off. We came to the street near my grandmother's house, and he turned the corner. It was obvious that we weren't going straight there. "So where have you been lately?" I asked, just to make conversation.

"So you sweatin' me now?"

"I just asked you a question. It's no big deal," I huffed.

"I'm just stressin'. I had to take care of some business."

"Business, like from last weekend?"

"Yeah."

"That guy you left the club with, what happened to him?"

"I don't know," he lied.

"He got stabbed, right?"

He pulled the car to a smooth stop at a traffic signal then looked over at me and shrugged. "He deserved it, no vital organs."

"Isn't that kind of cold? I thought he was a friend."

"He's a business associate who needs to step up."

So, instead of going straight to my grandmother's house or even staying in D.C., he headed over to Montgomery County. He said he needed to drop off something at his friend's house. About fifteen minutes later we pulled up in front of this townhouse. He got out and went inside. A few minutes later he came out. "Hey, come on in for a minute."

"Why? I need to get home."

"Come on. I want to introduce you to a friend of mine."

I got out and followed him into the house. We went into the kitchen. There were two girls standing at the counter. They looked like they'd just walked off the set of a rap video. One had on a micromini with a fishnet top and black bra, and the other had on tight shorts and a low cut shirt. I looked totally out of place. "A'ight, Kenisha, this is Dantee. He's a friend."

"Hi," I said half smiling, looking him directly in the eyes. He, on the other hand was checking out my breasts.

"She a'ight man. She is pretty. You should have her stop by the party tomorrow and make friends. She like to dance, right?"

"Oh, yeah, she can dance. She go to one of those dance schools in D.C. She can seriously dance, and she has friends who dance, too. Yo, yo, man, she know Tyrece Grant, too. Gonna hook a brotha up." They bumped fists. I just shook my head.

"Get out, she know Tyrece? That's tight. Yeah, bring her to the party tomorrow night. She can dance. If she any good, she can stop by the club after that."

"Excuse me, I'm standing right here," I said sarcastically. Dantee and the two girls standing there looked at me, then at Darien. "What?" I asked but nobody said anything. They just started talking about something else.

I stood right there while they talked like I wasn't there. Talk about being ignored. I didn't say anything more, but hell, no, there was no way I was coming to no stupid party here tomorrow night or any other night. All I wanted to do now is go home. Darien finally finished his business, and the guy reminded him again to bring me to the party before we left.

We were walking back to the car, and I just had to say something to him. "So at what point did I not exist in there? You and your friend were talking like I wasn't even on the planet, let alone in the room."

"That's how he do," he said, as if that was an explanation.

"Well, it's rude and disrespectful. You keep talking about how you want respect. Well, you need to learn how to show respect, too."

"Whatever, so let's go over to my dad's crib. He's away, but we can hang out."

"No thanks," I said. "I need to get home and do homework."

"Don't be stressing all that studying stuff."

"I need to get home," I repeated again. The tone in my voice was unmistakable. I was pissed and he knew it.

He sighed loud and long, like I was messing up his world or something. Truthfully, I really didn't care. It was a long day, a long week, and all I wanted to do was go home and chill. After much debate and cussing under his breath, Darien finally dropped me off down the street from my grandmother's house. I could tell he was pissed, but I really didn't care. I needed to seriously rethink this whole hanging out with Darien thing. He was in a whole other league than me. Drugs, alcohol, violence, Darien was moving way too fast. Keeping up with him was crazy.

When I walked up the street, I saw my dad's car parked out front. I was so glad I made Darien drop me off down the street. I walked up the brick path. My dad and grandmother were standing on the porch talking. "Hey, there she is," my dad said.

"Hi, Grandmom. Hey, Dad," I said hugging him. "I didn't know you were stopping by today."

"I stopped by to see my favorite girl, although you almost missed me. Where were you?"

"I stayed after school."

"Detention?" he asked, suddenly looking concerned.

"No, it's something like an advanced English lit class. I was bored in the regular class, so the teacher put together this accelerated class. It's pretty tight. I like it. He teaches stuff like at Hazelhurst, but it's mostly self study."

"I'm going to start dinner. James, you sure you can't stay a while longer and join us?" my grandmother asked.

"No, but maybe next time," Dad said, as my grandmother went back inside the house.

"So, how's Penn Hall treating you?"

"Fine, I took the Hazelhurst admissions exam last Saturday."

"How do you think you did?"

I crossed my fingers. "Hopefully I nailed it."

He nodded. "Good, now that's what I want to hear. Congratulations, I'm proud of you. Well, I gotta get home. Why don't you stop by this weekend? The boys are looking forward to seeing you. Oh and bring your friend."

"What friend?" I asked, hoping he wasn't talking about Cassie, since we really hadn't talked much since Ursula's party. All of a sudden she was hanging with Sierra. Strange.

"Terrence," my dad said.

"Terrence?" I asked.

"That's right. Your father knows a little something that's going on in your life. Why don't you two come up to the house Saturday? I'd like to meet this new boyfriend."

"Dad, it's not even like that."

"What's it like then," he asked.

"We're friends, buddies, that's it."

"Fine, I'd like to meet your friend, buddy, that's it."

"Dad," I moaned, hoping that would move him to change his mind. Apparently it didn't 'cause he just smiled at me blankly. "Well, see, he just came off line, so I don't know what he's doing this weekend."

"I know what he's doing. He's coming to the house."

"I'll see, okay, maybe."

"All right, I have to go." He leaned in and kissed my forehead. "Be good and listen to your grandmother. I'll see you Saturday, baby girl."

I waited until he drove off. Then, I picked up my book bag and went inside. I usually either head straight to my bedroom or to the kitchen, but this time for some reason I stopped in the living room. I plopped in the closest chair and just sat there. I looked up at the pictures on the wall. My crazy family was looking down at me.

My grandmother once told me that my past becomes my future. At the time I had no idea what that meant. She was also talking about seeing other people standing on land mines. I didn't get that either then, but now I think I was beginning to see what she meant. Maybe it was because I was reading and analyzing Langston Hughes or something but I was starting to understand what she was talking about. It was a perception thing.

What's crazy or unorthodox to some might be perfectly sane to others. I wondered about that then remembered what Diamond, Jalisa and Li'l T said. Maybe they were the ones seeing clearly. Was I all messed up?

I heard my grandmother walking down the hall from the kitchen. She was headed upstairs, then seeing me, she stopped and came into the living room. "Was it that kind of day?" she asked, sitting on the sofa across from me.

"I think it's that kind of life," I said.

"What's going on?" she asked.

I shook my head. There was nothing to say. I knew she wouldn't get it. She's sixty-something years old and stays in church all the time. There's no way she'd understand my drama. I don't even understand my drama. "Nothing," I muttered.

"On the contrary, it's definitely something. Anytime you're going to sneak out of my house in the middle of the night to hang out with some boy, it's something."

Okay. I think I stopped breathing. "Grandmom…"

"Denial would be insulting to both of us, so don't," she said.

Damn. "Yes, I snuck out Saturday night," I said, quietly. "I'm sorry."

"No, Kenisha, you're not contrite. You got caught. You're sorry about that, fine. But it's not about sneaking out. It's about trust and respect. You messed up. You lost both."

I closed my eyes then opened them slowly. This wasn't the same as when my mom was alive. I never snuck out of the house, but sneaking in was always a breeze. "So, you don't trust or respect me anymore?" I asked.

"It's not about me, Kenisha, it's about you. Given what you did, do you trust or respect yourself, your ability to make sound choices and good decisions?"

"The choices we make are the choices we live with." I heard myself repeating my mother's mantra.

"Exactly. Can you live with the choices you've made lately?"

"I don't know."

"Yes, you do. You've been spiraling around here like a spinning top out of control, bumping into things, stumbling, but still spinning faster and faster. You know that won't last."

"But it's different here. It's not the same as before."

"No, it's not, but right is right, no matter where you are. Don't use that as an excuse."

She was blocking. Every time I said something, she blocked me out. "I was wrong," I said simply. She nodded silently. "So what happens now, I'm grounded?" I asked.

"Will that change anything?" she asked.

"No, but I did learn that it's disrespectful both to you and to myself to do what I did. And I am sorry. I won't do that again, I promise."

"Good."

"Pearls of wisdom?" I asked.

"No," she said, standing, "just plain old common sense."

Later, after dinner, I just sat in my bedroom chilling. There wasn't anything interesting on TV, so I went online and started surfing the Web. I looked up Terrence's fraternity at Howard. I checked to see what Tyrece and Gayle were doing. I looked up next week's schedule at Freeman Dance Studio and then checked out what was happening at Hazelhurst. While reading the school's latest newsletter, I got a message from my sister. I clicked on to visual.

I saw Jade's smiling face and instantly felt better. Funny,

I would have never thought I'd say something like that, but it was true. She was my connection to our mom and I was hers. We were like the only two people on this planet who could say that. It was good knowing that I wasn't alone.

"Hi, Jade," I said happily.

"Hey, what up?"

"Nothing, I was just chilling and surfing."

"No homework?"

"Nah, I did it all. I took the Hazelhurst exam last week."

"Good, how do you think you did?"

"I don't know. Good I hope. I'm ready to go back to school."

"What about the fighting?" she asked.

"Been there, done that, I've had enough."

"I heard," she said.

"You heard what?" I asked.

"I heard that you were at the go-go club last weekend."

"How did you find out? Grandmom told you?"

"No, but she knows of course. Believe me, you can't get anything past her. She may be old but she'd good, so don't even think that you got away with something."

"She already talked to me about sneaking out…"

"You snuck out too? Are you crazy? Do you know how dangerous that is? Anything could have happened to you…"

"…I know, I know, it was stupid and yes, Grandmom already talked to me about being irresponsible and disrespectful."

"Good, but seriously Kenisha, you can't be doing stuff like that. It's too dangerous. I used to go to the go-go clubs too, and like clockwork some fool would act up and the police would be all over the place. Don't get caught up in all that drama."

"Yeah, I see that now."

"Who did you go with?"

"Some friends. I got a ride there and back. I saw a few fights but stayed as far away from the rest of the stuff as possible."

"Good, I don't know why there's always one idiot who has to mess it up for everybody."

"Tell me about it."

"I heard on the news that there was a stabbing."

"Yeah" was all I said, I didn't want to go into detail and let her know that I was too close to everything. "So how's Tyrece?"

"Good. He's in the studio now."

"A new CD?"

"He's working on it."

"Are you going to be on it?"

"As what, a singer? Girl, you must have bumped your head at the go-go the other night. You know the only way I can carry a tune is in a bucket of water. I can't sing."

I laughed. We started talking about colleges and which ones I was interesting in attending. She gave me some helpful hints. Then we talked about just about everything else. She asked about Diamond and Jalisa, and I gave her vague answers. Then she asked about lawn mower guy. I told her that he crossed over on line. She was genuinely happy for him. I kind of wished I'd been happy for him too now. I shouldn't have been so distant and upset, but it was too late. I doubted seriously that he'd come home this weekend. Maybe I'd call him later tonight. But I doubt that, too. Maybe Friday.

seventeen

All Hell Breaks Loose

"It's a fundamental paradox of life. Bad things happen to good people. Or is it good things happen to bad people? Either way...somebody gets screwed."
—MySpace.com

Friday came quicker than I expected. All of a sudden it was here. I have no idea what happened to Wednesday and Thursday. I guess I just sleepwalked the days away 'cause I seriously don't remember them. So it was the weekend now. School was over, and I was so ready to get out of the "Penn." I grabbed a few books from my locker and started checking the list I made during my last class period. This weekend was crucial. I needed to buckle down and hit the books hard. I was caught up with assignments, but I needed to study.

"Hey Kenishiwa. What you doing tonight?"

What an ass. I didn't even look up. I knew who it was. There was only one fool dumb enough to consistently call me something as ridiculous as Kenishiwa. I don't know if he thought it was funny or cute, but it was definitely annoying. But given his limited mentality, he probably thought it was my real name.

"Do you even have any idea what you're actually saying when you call me that?" I asked. He looked stumped. "Do any of you know? Do you even know what language it is?" He grimaced as if his brain were about to implode. "Never mind," I said, "don't hurt yourself."

So as usual Troy was standing there spouting some crap that he hoped would get me to go out with him, which probably meant going someplace and dropping my panties. Not. I swear, the redundancy of his drama is so meaningless. The fact that he actually believes that his nonsense and stupidity will wear me down is insulting. I just looked at him and shook my head. To think that Troy, this wasted lump of flesh, had actually received a five-year scholarship to college. It was insane. Just because he could toss an object a few yards, he was given a full ride. They'd better make it eight years since everyone knew that Troy had the IQ of a meat loaf, and that was a major insult to the meat.

So anyway, I shot him down, as per our usual dance of wasted time. He and his friends walked away as usual, laughing and slapping each other on the back. I just stood there at the open locker and shook my head. I know I'm about to sound like my grandmother but, "Lord save me from this stupidity."

I noticed that one of his friends stayed back. He walked up to me and cleared his throat. I turned around and glared at him, waiting for something stupid to come out of his mouth. This is all I needed this week, another Troy wannabe.

"You better go and catch up with your friends," I said, trying not to add another smart remark to the rebuff.

"We're not exactly friends, more like teammates."

I looked up. "I know you, right?" I asked.

"Yeah, my name's Barron James. We hung out and danced at Ursula's party the other night. Girl, you can really dance, Freeman, right?"

"Yeah, you're not too bad yourself. Do you go to Freeman?"

"Nah, I just hang around picking up stuff as I go."

I nodded impressed. "Not bad for just hanging around."

"Thanks, um, listen, don't be too upset with Troy. He's just trying to impress the guys."

"Yeah, I get that. I just don't like being the target all the time," I said, then looked at him suspiciously. "What about you, you trying to impress the guys, too?"

"Nah," he said.

"You know if he calls me Kenishiwa one more time I swear I'm gonna jump up and strangle him."

He laughed. "So, I guess I shouldn't tell you that the nickname Kenishiwa was kinda my idea, huh?"

"Your idea?" I said, surprised for some reason.

"Well, see *konichiwa* is Japanese. It's a greeting meaning, like hello or how are you? So it seemed kinda tight to blend your name and the Japanese word. Kenishiwa."

Damn, I was impressed, a football player with an actual brain. "That's pretty good, smart play on words," I said smiling. "So who told you what it meant?"

"My dad's in the military. We were stationed in Japan for a few years. We moved to D.C. a year ago."

"Do you miss Japan?" I asked.

"Yeah, it was nice. My grandparents are still there, and I'm supposed to go back and visit next year. I'm looking forward to it." I nodded seeing the hint of Asian facial features. He was nice looking. A little thin but he seemed cool. "Um, listen, I was meaning to ask you something."

"What?"

"Um, are you doing the Halloween thing tonight?"

"Halloween," I asked, completely forgetting about it, again. "Oh, right, I completely forgot. No, I'm not going out, you?"

"Yeah, I'm taking my niece and nephew out tonight."

"Awe, that's nice," I said sincerely.

He started telling me about what they were wearing, but I wasn't listening anymore. I was wondering about my two half brothers. They were at the perfect age to enjoy Halloween. I wondered what they'd be dressed as tonight—knowing them probably something crazy. I should be there with them, helping them with their costumes, taking them around the neighborhood; but I wasn't. I promised myself that I'd go online later and at least see their outfits.

"So, at Ursula's party the other night, you were there with those two girls, right?"

"Yeah, Jalisa and Diamond. They're my best friends. Why?" I asked smiling, knowing that he must have been interested in one of them.

"Nah, nothing," he said shyly, looking away smiling. "I was just curious. Which one is which?"

"Jalisa has the braids, and Diamond has straight black hair."

"Diamond, huh, she like seeing anybody now, I mean like that guy she was dancing with at the party?"

"No, not that I know of. Why, are you feeling her? Do you want me to introduce you?"

"Nah, that's okay. Well maybe, I guess. Sure."

"A'ight, let me talk to her, then I'll let you know. She lives in Virginia in my old neighborhood, but we hang out at Freeman sometimes."

"Yeah, I know. That's where I saw her before."

My brow arched. It seemed that Barron was seriously liking Diamond. I kinda like the look of them together. They'd make a cute couple. "So, I'll talk to her and let you know, okay."

"A'ight," he said smiling as he backed up to leave. "I gotta go anyway. Football practice is in ten minutes."

"You're on the football team?"

"Actually mostly the track team. I'm a sprinter. Some of us do football, too."

"A'ight, see ya." After he left I couldn't stop smiling. It was so cool that he asked about Diamond. Most guys interested in Diamond were either too intimidated by her looks or her dancing ability or they were just plain jerks.

"Kenisha."

I turned the other direction. My current frenemy, Cassie, was standing there smiling ruefully at me. I obliged her with a halfhearted smirk. "Hey, Cassie," I said still going through my locker.

"So, you talkin' to him now?" she asked.

"Who?" I asked looking at her. "Eww, are you okay? You look kinda bad."

"I'm okay. I just got a cold I think," she said sniffing.

"Maybe you should see a doctor about it or something."

"Well, maybe it's sinus or allergies, I don't know."

"Still, you should get that checked out," I said.

"So you talking to him or what?"

"Barron, no. He asked about one of my girls from Virginia. I'm gonna introduce them."

"Oh, 'cause I thought you was with D."

"I am not with Darien. We're friends and that's all. You know I'm talking to Terrence."

"Oh, right, so what are you doing tonight?" she asked.

"I don't know yet, probably studying. Why?"

"But it's Halloween. You gotta hang out tonight," she said.

"I don't think so."

"Come on, I heard about this really nice party tonight. I don't want to go by myself. Want to go with me?"

"Nah, I really need to study."

"Can't you study tomorrow? It's supposed to be really fun," she cajoled.

Now here's the thing: I don't trust Cassie anymore. She used to be my around-the-way girl, but now my gut was telling me that she was a hater and a faker. I don't know, there's something about seeing her hanging with Sierra that seemed strange, especially since she told me she couldn't stand her anymore. She was two-faced, yeah, I got that, but there was something else. I don't know. "Nah, it's important, I need to study all weekend."

"A'ight, you going home now?"

"No, I need to stop by my English lit class and pick something up. I don't know how long it's gonna take."

"A'ight, see you later."

"Yeah, later," I said. After she left, I grabbed what I needed from my locker and slammed it tight. I went to my class and picked up my Langston Hughes essay. I talked to the teacher about it. He really liked it, and he even suggested I consider using it as a platform for my college essay. I walked out the school building feeling pretty great for the first time in a long time.

I didn't see anybody on the way home. That was good. I went home and showed my grandmother my essay. She was impressed and that really made me feel good. She suggested I tell Jade since Langston Hughes was her favorite poet. I immediately e-mailed her a copy of the essay. I cooked dinner and hung out with my grandmother awhile. It was warm out so we sat on the front porch talking about her fall plants, school and the upcoming holidays. It wasn't time for bingo at the church yet, so we were just sitting back chilling and handing out treats.

"So, what are you doing this evening?" she asked.

"Nothing. I have homework and studying to do, that's all."

"No parties?"

"Nah, I'm kind of putting that on hold for awhile."

She nodded slowly but didn't say anything more.

Later, after my grandmother left for bingo, I went upstairs and sat down at the computer table. I grabbed my cell and turned it off so that I could study without interruption. I read a few chapters of a history assignment, finished a chemistry worksheet I'd started earlier and then opened my trigonometry textbook. I for real didn't feel like doing trig, so I went online to check out the current Hazelhurst assignment site. As I was going through the listed information, I got an IM. It was from Diamond.

"Help! Help! The mayor and good people of Another-townsville, USA need our help. Professor What's-His-Name has been kidnapped by the Meanies. They threaten to slice off his sideburns if we don't bring them the secret chemical ZYX formula!"

There was also a badly drawn sketch and a ransom note. I laughed so hard tears rolled down my cheeks. I was just about to send a reply when I got an IM and camera message. It was Jalisa. I really didn't feel like talking, but I clicked over anyway.

Jalisa was sitting there with Diamond beside her. They were dressed like two of the Powerpuff Girls. It was our costume from last year—Blossom, Bubbles, the only one missing was Buttercup, me. "Hey," I said smiling happily as if everything was all right with us.

They didn't speak. Instead they held up a piece of paper with words written on it, "We're still mad, and we're not talking to you."

"Okay," I said slowly.

They changed to another piece of paper. It read, "Hi!"

I shook my head. They are so crazy. "Hi," I said smiling again.

Another paper, "Did you get our message from before?"

I laughed. "You mean about the professor?" I asked.

They looked at each other and then quickly grabbed a marker and another piece of paper. Jalisa scribbled something fast and Diamond held it up. "Yes."

I laughed again. "Yeah, I got the message," I said.

They scrambled for another sheet of paper, then finding it, held it up. "The professor is okay, but his sideburns are gone. The Meanies are in jail."

"So y'all didn't need me," I said.

Another piece of paper said, "I know you might still be mad at us too, and maybe we're not talking, but we wanted you to know that we miss you. Two Powerpuff Girls just doesn't seem right."

"I miss y'all," I said sadly, "and I'm not mad. I was just tripping before. I'm sorry."

They found another piece of paper. "We're sorry, too."

"So are we talking now?" I asked.

They dropped the rest of the papers. "Yeah," they said in unison. "Guess what we did tonight?" Diamond asked quickly. Of course I knew the answer. Ever since we were old enough, we went trick-or-treating together. First with Natalie, Jalisa's older sister, and then when we were old enough we hung out by ourselves. Together we'd been everything from the three little pigs to the Three Stooges. But last year was the best.

"Let me think," I said, then paused. "Trick-or-treating?"

"We took my nieces and a few neighborhood kids out earlier. Now we're hitting a party. You're invited, too," Jalisa said.

"Nah, I really need to chill and hit the books. The

Hazelhurst exam was last week, and if I passed I still have to be ready to start next semester."

"How do you think you did?" Jalisa asked.

"She aced it," Diamond said confidently.

"I aced it, I hope," I said. They cheered.

"A'ight wait, so what happened to you. We called you like a dozen times before," Jalisa said.

"Yeah, we were gonna pick you up to go trick-or-treating."

"Sorry, I turned my cell phone ringer off. I think it's still on off," I said, picking it up and changing the setting.

"Oh, Diamond, before I forget, there's somebody who wants to meet you," I said.

"Who?" she asked skeptically.

"He saw you at Ursula's party last weekend."

"Why didn't he say something to me then?" she asked.

"I don't know? I guess he was just checking you out."

"So who is it?"

"Remember that guy I was dancing with?" I said.

"Him?" she asked. Jalisa started laughing. "Are you kidding me?" she continued, then crinkled her nose and shook her head.

"Yeah, what's wrong with him? He's nice. He goes to my school. He used to live in Japan." She shook her head again. "What? What's wrong with him?"

"He's gangsta, definitely not my type," she said, "you know that. I can't deal with all that drama."

"No he's not. He's nice. He runs track, and he's on the football team. Believe me, he definitely isn't gangsta. He told me that he was checking you out at Freeman, too."

"And that's supposed to make me feel better?" she asked.

"Ew, stalker alert," Jalisa joked and laughed.

"Since when are you a snob, Diamond," I asked.

"Since 'Mr. He's-not-a-gangsta' walked out then came back into the party stinking like beer, cigarette and joint."

"No, he didn't. I don't even remember him going outside."

"He went outside with you, Kenisha."

"No he didn't. Wait, I'm not talking about Ursula's brother. I'm talking about the second guy I was dancing with. He's tall, brown skin, has nice eyes and he's quiet. Oh, and he can dance, too."

"Oh, I remember him," Jalisa said. "He had the shorts on."

"Yeah, that's him," I said.

"Oh, him," Diamond said. "Oh, he was kinda cute. I thought you were talking about that other guy. The one you went outside with. For real girl, Jalisa and I were two seconds from going out to make sure you were okay. Dude looked too gangsta."

"For real, Kenisha, he looked like bad news. I know he's your friend's brother and all but…"

"Don't worry about it. He is bad news," I said looking away. "Anyway, the guy I'm talking about is nothing like Darien. His name is Barron and he's really nice. He's funny. He calls me Kenishiwa."

"What?" they both asked.

"Yeah, it's like a play on my name and the Japanese word for hi, Kenisha and *konichiwa*."

"Real cute," Jalisa said, sarcastically.

"It is cute. Don't be hating," Diamond said. "At least he has a sense of humor."

"But Barron. His name is Barron," Jalisa said laughing. "Ew, what kind of name is that?"

"What's wrong with Barron? I like that name," Diamond said.

"Whatever," Jalisa said. I laughed. The conversation continued then veered off in all directions. We spent the next half hour talking, laughing and joking. It was like we were never mad at each other.

Afterward, I sat on my bed, opened my trigonometry book again and tried to concentrate. I started working a problem, but I guess I fell asleep 'cause I jumped when my cell rang. The shock of suddenly hearing Missy Elliott rapping startled me. I thought I upped the setting to vibrate but I guess not. I seriously have to change that ring tone back to hip-hop. I grabbed it off the desk and checked the caller ID. It was Darien's phone number. I didn't answer, and he didn't leave a message. I changed the setting to vibrate, then a few seconds later it rang again. It was Cassie calling. I answered. "Hello."

"Kenisha, you need to talk to your girl Ursula now. She's trippin' big time, for real."

"What, why, what's wrong?" I asked.

"I don't know, I just heard that something was up, and she was about to get in big trouble."

"Where is she?"

"I gotta go." She hung up.

I shook my head. It was sad. Cassie definitely wasn't

the person I thought she was. She was mean-spirited and manipulative. And trusting her was questionable. But still, Ursula had never done anything. She included me and had been nice to me—even to my friends. If she was in trouble, the least I could do was find out if she was okay and if I could help.

I walked over to Cassie's house and rang the doorbell. No one answered. I rang the bell again. "Nobody's home." Someone yelled from inside.

"I'm looking for Cassie," I said. The door opened. Her younger sister told me that she wasn't home and was probably with Darien. I wondered about that.

"Oh, right, I forgot that she was back to seeing Darien again," I said, hoping for more information.

"They never stopped," she snapped pointedly.

I headed down the street to Ursula's house. I saw Li'l T. It was late, but he was still out trick-or-treating. We talked as we walked.

I got to Ursula's house and Li'l T kept going. I rang the bell. Darien opened the door and just stood there. He didn't say anything. I really didn't feel like dealing with his drama, so I just ignored him.

"Where's Ursula?" I asked. He shrugged. His eyes were all glassy, and I could tell he was high. "Not funny, Darien. Cassie said that she was in trouble. Is she home or what?"

He shrugged then stepped back. I walked inside and called out to her. She didn't answer. I went into the living room and looked around. Their mother wasn't home, as usual. "So where's Ursula?" I asked again.

"I don't know. She's not here, I guess." He was smiling like he knew something I didn't. He glanced upstairs.

I could tell he was lying. I went to the stairs and called up to her, but she didn't answer. I went up to her bedroom. I knocked on the closed door then opened it and looked inside. She wasn't there. I was on my way back downstairs when I heard a female laughing in Darien's bedroom. I figured it was Ursula, so I walked down the hall and went in. It was Cassie. She was lying across the bed watching TV. As soon as I walked in, she jumped up. She looked just as high as he did.

"She's here, now gimmie my stuff, I gotta go," she said to Darien. He tossed her a tiny Ziploc bag from the small pile on the dresser by the door. She grabbed it off the bed and left.

I saw some more baggies and the thin lines of white powder beside them. It was obvious that they had been getting high together. I also saw a gun. I didn't need this. "Y'all are so stupid," I said, shaking my head. Of all the things to do, getting high was the dumbest. I headed out right behind Cassie, but then all of the sudden Darien blocked the doorway. "Move Darien," I said firmly.

"So, we hanging tonight, or what? We can party here then go to Maryland to my friend's house."

"No, we aren't hanging out tonight. I already have plans tonight, so get out the way. Move! I'm not playing Darien. Move."

"You promised my friend, Dantee, that you would go to his party and dance for him."

"Oh, please, do you really think I'm going to some

party at that house? Get real. And I didn't promise anything. You did. So you go dance for him," I snapped, and then tried to push by him. He grabbed my arm and yanked me back. He was high, but apparently he was still focused. The look in his eyes scared the hell out of me. I was in trouble, and getting past him was my only way out. "Look Darien, this isn't funny. I don't feel like playing games with you."

"Games, oh, girl please, you the queen of games. You're always playing games, trying to tease somebody. TB might like that tight-ass virgin shit, but I'm not down with it."

"I never teased you," I said. He didn't say anything. He just looked me up and down. "Terrence is coming over tonight," I said quickly, hoping that might make him move. It didn't.

"You think I care about TB?"

"You should."

"I bet his punk-ass never told you what he did to me."

"He didn't do anything to you," I said.

Darien laughed. "That punk-ass bitch stabbed me." He took off his shirt. The scar on his shoulder was there. I remembered it from before. "He damn-near punctured my lung."

"You're lying," I said.

"Nah, baby," he said, smiling again. "Why don't you get comfortable? Sit down, chill."

"I told you I have to go. Terrence is..."

"Yeah, yeah, TB is coming over. I think we both know better than that. See, me and TB go back a few years. We were in juvie together."

"What?"

"That punk-ass wannabe ain't tell you he was in juvie?" He started laughing again.

"I know about that. Somebody killed his brother."

"I stabbed his brother so he stabbed me."

"Oh, shit," I said. It all made sense. Terrence once told me that he was sent to juvenile hall for stabbing the guy who killed his little brother. Darien was that guy.

"Why don't you take off your clothes?"

"Why don't you drop dead?" I said, absolutely meaning it.

"See, you teasing me again. I'm tired of it. You acting like you all Goody-Two-shoes better than everybody. You ain't better than me. See, my dad was a football player, too. I got the hook-up." He took a step toward me. I backed up and looked around. He reached for my arm. I snatched it away. He grabbed the front of my shirt just as I moved away. He scratched me as my shirt half ripped down the front. He smiled. "That's more like it."

"You need to back off, Darien, before you get hurt," I warned, hoping he'd buy it. He was much bigger than me, so there was no way I could get away without him catching me first. The only thing to do was to take him down. I thought about grabbing the gun, but instead I turned and grabbed one of his stupid trophies just as his hand touched my shoulder. I swung around fast. He obviously didn't expect to see the gold-plated trophy turning with me. His eyes got wide just before it connected with his face.

eighteen

Speeding Bullet

"When you're autonomous, you stand alone. The guideposts of life turn away, leaving you without direction. But that doesn't mean you stop moving forward. You keep going as fast as you can until somehow, someway, life makes sense again."

—MySpace.com

"**Bitch!**" He let go of my shoulder and then stumbled back. His face was bleeding, and the trophy broke into four pieces. Holding the side of his face, he looked at me and I knew, for real, I was through. But I swear, I wasn't going out by myself. He started toward me again.

I reached back, grabbed another trophy and swung it. Seeing it coming, he blocked it with his arm. I heard a crack. "Bitch!" he yelled again. I dropped the second broken trophy and grabbed another one. I turned, ready. He stopped coming at me. He'd staggered back against the side wall bending down hunched over. I wasn't about to wait around to see if he was okay. I got out of there fast. I jumped down the steps like four at a time. My shirt was flying open as I ran out the front door. My bra was showing, but I didn't even care.

The first person I saw was Li'l T, but I didn't stop. He called my name, but I wasn't hearing him. He must have been running right behind me, because I heard him telling me to wait. I never ran track in school because of my asthma, but make no mistake I can run when I need to. I was at my grandmother's house instantly. I unlocked the door. I made it. I was safe. Before I could turn the knob I felt somebody grab me from behind. "Kenisha, what's happened?"

There was no trophy, but I swung anyway. My fist barely grazed the side of something solid. I missed. Somebody grabbed me and held tight. "Get off!" I screamed as loud as I could then swung out again. This time I hit something.

"Damn, she hit me!"

"Kenisha, chill. It's me."

"Did you see that? See, see, I told you, she's crazy. Let her go. He got her man, see, told you."

"Kenisha stop, it's me, Terrence."

"Get off me," I yelled again.

"It's me, lawn mower guy," Terrence repeated, still holding tight. Through the muffled sounds of the struggle, I heard him. I stopped fighting and started crying.

"What happened to you? Who did this?"

I just shook my head. Breathing and talking was too hard, so I just kept shaking my head.

"Come on. Let's go inside," Terrence said.

We went into the living room and sat down. It was still

difficult to breathe, but I was a lot calmer knowing that Terrence was with me. He called out to my grandmother, but she wasn't home yet. "Where's your inhaler?" he asked. I pointed to my pocketbook on the chair. "Get the medicine." He instructed.

Li'l T grabbed my purse and started dumping everything out. I didn't even know he was there before. He dug through and found my inhaler. He gave it to Terrence, and then Terrence gave it to me. I inhaled twice, then instantly began to feel better.

"You okay?" Li'l T asked anxiously. I nodded slowly.

"Do you want some water?" Terrence asked. I nodded again. Li'l T jumped up and quickly headed out of the living room. I heard him walking down the hall toward the kitchen.

"All right, now tell me what's going on," Terrence said. "What happened to your shirt? Did you get robbed or something?"

"No, I was looking for one of my friends."

"Diamond and Jalisa are still outside?" he asked, just as Li'l T came back to living room. He handed me a mug of water. I took a sip and then a deeper swallow. The cool water eased down my throat, and I started feeling much better.

"Did you see Diamond or Jalisa tonight?" Terrence asked Li'l T. He shook his head, no.

"No, not them," I said. "I went to find Ursula, but…"

"Ursula?" Terrence asked and then looked at Li'l T.

"You remember her. They used to call her Ula, D's sister."

"You went over to D's house?" he yelled. I didn't say anything. "He did this?"

"Yeah, man. I saw her going there before, and then I saw her running out. I ran after her, and that's when you just saw us running up to the house."

Terrence didn't say anything after that. He just stood up and walked out. "Terrence wait, wait, it's not what you think. I wasn't hanging with Darien anymore. I was looking for Ursula, not him. He used Cassie to trick me into going over there. They told me that Ursula was in trouble," I said following him to the front door. I knew he was pissed with me. "Terrence, wait," I said, but he just stormed out and kept going.

"Crap." I looked at Li'l T and rolled my eyes. "Thanks for nothing," I said facetiously.

"What, hey, you just hit me and ain't nobody told you to hang with D. As a matter of fact I distinctly remember telling you that you need to chill with all that. But did you listen to me? Nooo. You didn't listen."

"Yeah, right, whatever, bye," I said, dismissing him. I moved out of the way then waited for him to leave, too.

"You're just mad 'cause you know I'm right."

"Are you leaving or what?" I asked.

"Yeah, but you ain't had to hit me like that," he sulked.

"I'm sorry, I thought you were—" I started then stopped, not wanting to even say his name anymore "—never mind."

"Yeah, fine, I'm going. But you do know where he's going don't you?" Li'l T asked.

"Who, Terrence? Yes, back to Howard," I said.

"Nah, he's going over to Darien's house," Li'l T said, smiling as he walked past me to the porch. "He's gonna kick D's ass."

"No, he's not," I said, then followed Li'l T out onto the porch. I looked down the street. From where I was, I could barely see Terrence. He was running down the street toward Ursula's house. He was just about already there. "Oh, shit. Darien's got a gun on his dresser. If Terrence gets hurt because of me..." I slammed the door then followed Li'l T running.

By the time we got there, Terrence and Darien were already outside fighting. Terrence was beating on Darien hard. All Darien could do was hold up one arm to fend him off. A few neighbors started gathering and then I heard sirens coming. Moments later a few people turned into a small crowd. People were yelling and screaming, but everybody was cheering for Terrence.

"Kick his punk-ass, TB. He needs it," somebody yelled.

"Yeah, kick his ass TB, like before. We got your back."

Darien looked around. His eyes were all glassy still. His face was swollen and he cradled his arm to his side. "Oh, so y'all all think y'all want a piece of me, too. A'ight, come on. Try it," he yelled angrily. He pulled out a knife and everybody took a step back. "You think you bad TB. That you can take me? Mess with this," he said swinging wide. Terrence jumped back. "Come on. You think you bad," he said, swinging again. Terrence avoided the blade a second time.

Darien circled and moved closer, somebody pushing him from behind. He swung around quickly. But that was all the distraction Terrence needed to knock him down. The knife slipped out of his hand, but before Terrence could hit him again, Sierra came out of nowhere and started kicking him. Darien was screaming by now, since each of her kicks landed on his cradled arm.

The crowd was really getting into it now. People were cheering and yelling. I looked away. I didn't want to see it anymore.

The police got there a few minutes later. They grabbed Sierra and pushed Terrence away. Another officer grabbed Darien. His arm crumbled. If it wasn't broken before, it was obviously broken now.

"Nah, nah, let TB kick his ass," somebody yelled.

"Yeah, he needs a beat down, punk."

"Y'all just jealous," Darien yelled at the crowd.

The officer put Darien in one car and Terrence in the other. They tried to tell everybody to go home. Of course nobody was listening to them. I tried to get to the police car with Terrence in it, but they weren't letting anyone close. By now another two police cars arrived and everybody started dispersing. But they were still talking about how Terrence beat Darien down.

While the police were distracted with the dispersing of the crowd, I got to see Terrence. He was sitting in the backseat with his head down. I called to him, but he didn't look up or answer. I called out louder. "Come on, let's go, let's go. Step back," an officer said to me.

I stepped away, but I knew he heard me calling him. A few minutes later the police car with Terrence in it drove away. He looked up. I just stood there not knowing what to do. Because of me, Terrence was headed to the police station. I looked around seeing people leaving, and then I saw Sierra standing there, too. The toe of her white sneaker was covered in blood. She didn't say anything. She just looked at me for a second and then turned and walked away.

I ran home.

at Dr. Tubbs

ay," I started
ed over and
her," I said

?

ow. I'm too
ed to do and
at Sierra, at
and even at

I got up and
eathing was
or was like
hole time I
ringing and

I closed my
louder and
be? It was
ball. I heard
ame called.
like Li'l T,
d to drown

s drowning
no use. I
pillow and

g to work. As a matter
as working pretty well.
st hope I don't need to

—MySpace.com

ard. The loud solid bang
house. I bolted, latched,
three locks tight. It was like
g out. Every part of my life
e on the other side of that
way from me as possible.
m and slumped down in the
feel was gone, and the pain
g to hurt again. The feeling
rrosive anger—ate at me. I
. An explosion was coming.
fight, but not to cry, no, not

again, never again. I started remembering wh
said, but he was wrong.

"No, it's not okay, it's not okay, it's not ok
whispering without even realizing it. I chan
over again. "No, it's not okay to be mad a
aloud.

But what if everybody was right all along

I need to stop. But I can't. I don't know l
angry, I'm too mad, at Darien for what he tr
Cassie for setting me up like that. I'm mad
Ursula, at Li'l T, at Diamond and Jalisa
Terrence and I don't even know why.

I grabbed my atomizer and inhaled deep.
went upstairs. My chest was heavy, and my b
labored. Climbing the stairs to the third fl
climbing a mountain straight up. Plus the
was going upstairs, I could hear the doorbel
then knocking on the front door.

I got to my room, lay on the bed and ther
eyes hoping it would stop. It didn't. It just g
louder. I knew it was Li'l T. Who else could
just like him to pester me still. I crawled into a
my cell vibrating and then I heard my r
Somebody was yelling in the street. It sounde
but I don't know. I put the pillow over my he
it out.

My head was spinning, and I felt like I w
in darkness. I tried to hold on, but it w
squeezed my eyes tight, held to the side of th
let the darkness cover me.

My medicine had done the trick. But I guess I took too much, 'cause when I do, and I'm already upset, I get dizzy and kind of pass out. It happened before, the night when my mom died. She slapped me, and I got mad then ran out the house. I don't remember anything much after that, but I guess Terrence brought me back. I was having trouble breathing, so my mom gave me the medicine. I guess it was too much 'cause I woke up in the same halfway haze then that I was in now.

But the good thing was that I was safe, calm and breathing better, even though things were still kind of foggy. I opened my eyes to see the time. My head was still spinning, so I closed them tight again. I remembered everything, Cassie, the drugs on the dresser, the gun and of course Darien and what he tried to do.

I still can't believe that I trusted his stupid ass. But even after everything, I was more upset with myself. It was so dumb of me to go into the house like that. I'd heard the lecture so many times from my mom about walking right into trouble. I can't believe I just did that. Stupid, stupid, stupid, I seriously know better, but I did it anyway. But out of everything that happened, I especially remembered Terrence and the disappointed look in his eyes as the police car drove away. The thing was, I didn't blame him one bit.

I opened my eyes slowly and looked straight up at the ceiling. The first thing I thought about was my mom. She had been looking out for me. I know she was with me the whole time. She must have given me the idea to hit him with the trophies 'cause I have no idea where it came from. All of a sudden I reached out and it was in my hand.

I miss her so much. I still can't believe she's gone sometimes. I get death. I know everybody's gotta go; it's inevitable. But that doesn't make it fair. It's been over two months. I guess I'll never stop missing her or loving her. After a while I just lay there, staring up, remembering, running, breathing and the banging on the front door. The haze in my head was clearing, and I started thinking about what almost happened. I got scared all over again. If he wasn't so high, if I hadn't grabbed the trophies, if I hadn't run fast enough…

My cell phone vibrated. I ignored it and looked across the room at the clock. I'd been asleep for an hour. I got up and went downstairs. The house was quiet and outside was quiet. It wasn't that late but I guess trick-or-treating was way over. I went to the front window and peeked through the curtain. Nobody was outside, and my grandmother's car wasn't in its usual space in front of the house. It wasn't unusual. Sometimes she stayed late after bingo to sit and talk with her friends.

I headed for the kitchen, and as soon as I turned the light on, the house phone rang. I almost jumped out of my skin as I grabbed it. "Hello."

"Kenisha, it's Dad. I've been trying to call you all night."

"It's on vibrate and I forgot to um—"

"I stopped by earlier, but no one was at home."

"I was—"

"Never mind about that. I need your help. I'm at the hospital. Courtney's in labor. She's early, and there are complications."

"What do you want me to do?" I asked.

"Yes, yes, I know, why should you even care? I know the two of you never got along, and it's understandable. It's my fault. I was wrong to do what I did, and how I did it, but all that is in the past. I can't change it. I wish I could. Your mother, everything. I wish I could just go back and make everything right again, but I can't and I..." he rambled.

"Dad, no, that's how I meant it. What do you want me to do to help?" I heard myself saying with all sincerity.

"Thank you. The boys are here with me. I need you to..."

"What hospital? I'll come get them," I said.

I wrote down the name of the hospital then called a cab. The dispatch said that it would be at least an hour's wait— maybe more—because of Halloween and all the Friday night parties in Georgetown. I called the only other person I could think of and then I left a quick note for my grandmother.

My ride came in no time, and within fifteen minutes, we arrived at the emergency area. It was packed. I couldn't believe all the people in there waiting. I found my dad and the boys sitting in the waiting area by the window. Dad was staring blankly at the TV, and the boys were curled up asleep in the same chair beside him.

We walked over, and he got up as soon as he saw us. I could see his eyes tearing. He grabbed us both and just held tight. Neither Jade nor I pulled away. "Thank you, thank you," he whispered.

"No thanks necessary," Jade said.

"How's Courtney and the baby?" I asked.

"She's asleep. They're trying to wait the problem out."

"Is that a good idea, I mean just sitting back doing nothing and hoping for the best?" I asked.

"Apparently," he said.

"How early is she?" Jade asked.

"Two months."

"How long has she been in labor?" she continued.

"I don't know. We fought and I walked out. When I got back, the boys had called the police because she'd fallen."

I looked over at the sleeping boys. Their heads were together, and they looked like little angels. I walked over and woke up them up. They grabbed me and held tight, each talking a mile a minute about what happened. "…and there was blood everywhere…" "…and she fell down…" "…I called 911 like in school, they taught us that and I remembered…" "…I know too…"

"All right guys, come on. Get your coats. You're coming home with me."

"To the gingerbread house?" Jason asked. I nodded. "Yeah," they yelled.

"Shh," I said holding my finger to my lips, "you have to be quiet, okay?"

"Okay," they each whispered. "Who's that?"

I knew they were talking about Jade, but I turned anyway. "That's Jade. She's my sister."

"We have another sister?" Jr. said.

"We have another sister?" Jason repeated.

"Yes, we have another sister," I said not ready to explain the nuances of our slightly twisted and blended family.

They immediately jumped down from the chair and ran

full speed directly to Jade. Thank goodness she'd finished her conversation with Dad and saw them charging her. They slammed full impact into her legs and held tight.

"Whoa," she said, staggering back but able to remain steady, "and who are these little guys?" She giggled as they continued to hold her legs and talk.

"We're you sisters, see?" Jason said, pointing to Jr.

"Oh, okay. I have two new sisters," she said.

"Yeah," Jason said.

"Yes," Jade corrected.

"No, that's not right. We're not your sisters. You're our sisters," Jr. corrected Jason and Jade.

"Oh, I see, so that would make you my…"

Jason looked at Jr., and they both looked at me. I shrugged. Then Jason yelled, "Brothers." We all quieted him. But he was too excited to have come up with the right answer.

"I was gonna say that," Jr. said quickly.

"But I said it first," Jason teased.

"Come on, guys, let's get out of here," I said.

"Are we going to your house too?" Jr. asked Jade.

"Yes, is that okay?" Jade said.

"Do you have more cookies?" Jason asked.

"I don't think so, but maybe if you're very good, we can ask my grandmother if we can make more."

Jason yawned. "How do you make cookies?" he asked, sleepily.

"I'll tell you tomorrow. Come on," Jade said.

"Is mommy coming, too?" Jr. asked.

"No, your mom's busy right now."

"What's she doing?" Jason asked.

"Why don't we get a good night's sleep, and then we'll talk about everything tomorrow. Okay?" Jade said. "Come on."

"Thank you, Jade," Dad said, his voice cracking. She nodded as she took their hands and headed toward the exit.

"Is there anything else you need?" I asked.

He shook his head. "No, thank you, baby girl. After everything, I don't know how…"

"Don't worry about anything. Grandmom's gonna love having the boys over. You know how she is. We'll take good care of them."

"I know you will. I gave Jade the house keys. You'll need to get clothes and stuff for them."

"Sure, don't worry. You just take care of Courtney. Give her my best, for real."

"I will."

"Bye, Dad," I said, then hugged him.

By the time I got to the car, Jason and Jr. were belted and secure in the backseat. "Ready?" Jade asked. I nodded. We drove to my dad's house to get the boys' clothing and overnight bags. We gathered everything and headed back to D.C. The boys fell asleep instantly.

"So how've you been?" Jade asked casually.

"I've had better days," I said.

"Your dad's girlfriend will be fine," she said.

"No, it's not that. Terrence was picked up by the police tonight, and I need to figure out a way to get him out."

twenty

An Incidental Subplot

> "'The faster I go, the behinder I get.' It's a stupid plaque hanging on the wall in the kitchen. I never got it until now. I thought that if I ran fast enough then maybe I'd get away from all that drama. I was wrong."
>
> —MySpace.com

"Terrence got picked up by the police? How? Why?" Jade said, obviously louder then she expected because she glanced in the rearview mirror to the backseat. I looked around, too. The boys were still asleep.

"He was fighting this guy, and the police came."

"That doesn't sound like Terrence, at least not anymore. A few years ago, yes, maybe, no, make that definitely."

"Why, what do you mean? What happened a few years ago?"

"That's when his brother was killed."

"I thought that happened a long, long time ago."

"No, it was maybe three or four years ago, something

like that. When his brother died, he was so angry nobody could get through to him. Counselors tried, his parents tried, his friends tried, everybody tried."

"But he's not angry anymore? What happened?"

"He really should be telling you this."

"No, tell me," I asked.

"Grandmom happened. One day he was throwing stones out back, and he broke her shed window. Grandmom was pissed so she marched next door and told him to get his butt over there and fix it. He blew her off, and she really went off on him. I don't know what else happened, but he fixed the shed window. Then she told him while he was at it to cut her grass and trim her rose bushes. He did, and I guess that was the end of that. They got close."

"So Grandmom helped him," I said.

She nodded. "Yeah, that's why I told you to talk to her. She's good. I call her sometimes just to vent. She's better than any shrink, believe me. So, are you still that angry?"

"I didn't think so, but I guess I am, kinda."

"I can't tell you to just get over it because I know it's not that easy. Your feelings are valid, but you need to find another way to channel them."

"When you were angry at me all those years, what did you do?"

"Dance," Jade said, then laughed and shook her head. "Girl, I wanted to strangle you so many times. Your attitude, your behavior, everything about you pissed me off. And I'm not even going to get started about your father."

"I know, and I'm so sorry about all that..."

"Hey, we've done the sorry thing before. All that is in the past. We're sisters, we're friends."

"I know, but not knowing for all those years what was really going on in my life, it was like I was there but not really. Does that make any sense?"

"Yes, it makes a lot of sense."

"For real, it's like I woke up from a dream and all of a sudden I have a sister, a different house, two little brothers and no mom."

"And that's who you're really mad at, isn't it?"

"No," I said quickly.

"Of course you are," she said.

"I am not, I'm not mad at Mom. Why does everybody think that? I'm not mad at her," I affirmed.

"Why not? I am. I'm mad at her."

"How can you be mad at her? She's dead," I said.

"So, that doesn't mean I can't still be pissed. Kenisha, I'm angry, too. I'm mad as hell that she left me like this. I go to pick up the phone and call her and then it hits me that she's not there anymore. I drive up to the house and expect to see her sitting waiting on the porch for us to hang out and she's not there. You ask how can I be mad, are you kidding me? How can I not be mad at her."

I glanced over at her as she drove. The streetlights illuminated her profile. She looked just like mom, just like me. And she was feeling exactly everything I was feeling. I started crying. "About Terrence, there's more to it than just that he was fighting this guy," I said. "He got arrested because of me."

"Why did Terrence get arrested because of you?"

I told her everything, the whole story including what I'd left out about the go-go club and seeing the gun and drugs on the dresser and what Darien tried to do to me. The more I talked the more I cried. Everything just poured out of me. Jade was quiet the whole time. Then when I finished she didn't say anything, but when she finally did, it wasn't what I expected.

"Sometimes when I think about it," she began, "all the things that will never happen, I get so mad I feel like exploding. I would have loved to get married and have my dad walk me down the aisle and my mother sitting there in the front row. I would have loved to put her first grandchild in her arms. I would have loved to tell her that she's coming to live with me and Ty and that she never has to worry about anything ever again. I would have loved to tell her that I love her one more time.

"But I can't. That's never going to happen, and it's hard to accept, but it is what it is. Nothing will change that, not me getting pissed and not you fighting and messing up your life. Yes, it makes me livid because it's so unfair. She died too young. There's so much more she would have loved to see, to do and to be. You think I'm not mad, that I don't want to fight or punch something. Girl please, you don't know the half of it."

She paused and grabbed a small pack of tissues from the compartment between the two front seats. She took a tissue and handed me a couple. I just broke down crying more.

"To tell you the truth, Kenisha, I don't know what all

this means. I don't have a clue. I guess it's all about the grand design. Like Grandmom says, it was God's will. Mom was supposed to die when she did, and that's all there is to it. Now we're supposed to mourn her then go on. But I think it's how we go on that's the free will part. What we choose to do as a result of the hand we've been dealt is up to us.

"All I know is that mom would never have wanted you to be like this. Hanging out all night in places you know you have no business going, dealing with some street punks and God knows what else. Don't you know when you do all that you're not only letting your family down but you're letting yourself down? You've been reckless, not just with your life, but with others' as well."

"I know. I'm sorry," I muttered still crying. The whole time she was talking, all I could think about was that Mom will never see that I wanted to change, and be different, better.

"It's not about sorry. It's about stepping up. You messed up, but you brought others down with you. That's wrong. You said there was a gun on the dresser in this boy's bedroom. Do you have any idea how bad all this could have gone?"

"I know, I'm sorry." I repeated, knowing that the words were pathetically inadequate at this point.

"Yeah, yeah, sorry, I get that. But words are cheap. It's all about what we do that matters. Now Terrence has to pay for what you did, your mess."

"But it was like you said, I was mad at Mom."

"Bullshit, Kenisha. Stop copping out. Take responsibility for your actions. **Being angry** because Mom's dead isn't an excuse so stop **acting like** it is."

"I didn't know he was **gonna** go over there."

"Kenisha, stop making excuses. Own up to your drama," she said, angrily now. "You were wrong. Own it and deal with it. You knew Terrence and this punk had issues. You just said so yourself when you told me all this."

She was right, and I knew it. I messed up and Terrence got caught up in it. I guess I knew it all along. It was just easier to be numb and pretend not to feel anything. I guess I need to own my mess.

"Jade, we need to get him out."

"I know."

"But I don't know how. What do I do?"

"We'll figure it out. Don't worry. We'll ask Grandmom."

"Grandmom? What can she do?"

"I don't know, nothing, maybe everything, I don't know."

I nodded absently, but I was still worried. I couldn't even imagine what Terrence was going through. We got home a few minutes later. Our grandmother was sitting up waiting for us. I carried Jason and Jade helped Jr. They were both so sleepy. We got them upstairs, took off their clothes and put them in the same bed in the room next to my grandmother's.

We all went downstairs, and I told my grandmother everything she didn't already know. Jade stood by my side the whole time.

"Kenisha, you know that the choices we make have consequences."

"I know," I said. But that was it. There was really nothing else I could say. I'd messed up, made bad choices and people around me were getting hurt. "I messed everything up, Terrence…"

"Terrence will be fine."

"No he won't. The police arrested him."

"No they didn't."

"I saw it, Grandmom," I said more emphatically.

"You saw him drive away in a police car, yes, but he wasn't under arrest. Now that other bad little boy, I can't say the same about him. Lord knows what mess he's gotten himself into."

"Wait, what do you mean, Grandmom? How do you know he didn't get arrested?"

"Sweetie, where do you think I been all night? He called his mom and grandmom when we were out celebrating my bingo winning with a slice of pie at the diner."

"So you already knew about it."

"There's not much I don't know about in this neighborhood."

"That's the truth," Jade said, grinning wide.

"You went to the police station?"

"Yes, we all did—the whole bingo crew. See, I have my running crew, too," she joked. Jade laughed, but I just needed to know what happened.

"Lord have mercy, as soon as eleven little old ladies walk into the police station looking for Terrence, they stepped right up. We even got the minister down there. My friend, Julia Carter, threatened to call her son."

"Who's her son?" I asked.

"The mayor of the city," Jade answered.

"Then Margret Griffin and Blanch Howell stepped up and that just about sealed it."

"Who do they know?"

"It's not who they know. It's about who they are," Jade said. "Mrs. Griffin sits on the city council and Mrs. Howell owns and writes for the local newspaper."

"Publicity of this sort isn't exactly what anyone wants."

"So what happens now with Terrence? If he's not arrested then when are they going to let him go?"

"Lord, what a night. First I win big at bingo and then all this. I don't know what's next. Hopefully the roof won't come down on us."

"Grandmom, what about Terrence?" I insisted, anxiously.

"Oh, he's fine, came home right after we did."

I took my first calm breath all night. Terrence was fine, that's all I needed to know.

"Now, as for you, Miss Thing..." my grandmother started.

I knew I was in trouble. Anytime my grandmother called me Miss Thing, I was in deep drama. I was right, but nothing she said wasn't anything I didn't already know and say to myself. I was over my head and wrong. So I sat still and listened. I had it coming.

After she'd finished we all went upstairs to our bedrooms. I changed and lay down but I couldn't sleep. My cell beeped with a text message. It was late, and I couldn't imagine who'd be texting me at this time. I considered just ignoring it and checking it out later, but after the evening I had, what else could happen? I grabbed my cell. It was from my dad.

-U R the 1st 2 no, Court had a girl. I can't wait 4 u 2 meet Barbra, she's beautiful!!-

I read the text twice. My feelings were all over the place. Actually I didn't know what I felt. I was happy for my dad, but I was sad, too. I wasn't his baby girl anymore. It was time for me to grow up. But I was really confused about Courtney. All the drama she had with my dad and she still agreed to name their baby after my mother. I guess she'd still do whatever it takes to hold on to him.

I just shook my head. Everything that happened Halloween night would stay with me for a long time. I sat on the windowsill and looked out at the sky, and just waiting for whatever was coming next.

twenty-one

Slowing Down 2 Begin Again

"I think I've been running so fast that I outran myself. One minute ago was a month ago, and a month ago was forever ago. The obstacles I hurdle in my life continued to mount. I jumped but not high enough. I need to fly, I need to soar."

—MySpace.com

It was dawn. I'd been up all night, but it didn't feel like it. Usually when I stay up late studying or something, I'm sleepy and drowsy the next day, but today I felt pretty good. Everyone was still asleep, so I made myself a cup of hot tea and headed out on the front porch. As I passed the table in the front hall, I saw an envelope addressed to me. It was from Hazelhurst Academy. I guess after everything that happened last night I missed seeing it there.

I picked it up and considered what to do. I knew it was my test results, and I knew opening it meant I'd either go back or stay where I was. I glanced around, I was alone, but it was okay. I opened the letter and read the contents.

Afterward, I placed it back on the table for my grandmother and Jade to read. Then I went outside.

The early morning air was crisp and cool, much different than how it had been the past few weeks. It felt like fall was finally here. It felt good, like a change was coming.

I had my recipe book with me. I sipped my hot tea, sat down and flipped through the pages. I began reading some of the old entries. A lot of them were pretty good.

I called it my recipe book, and it did have some recipes in it, but it also had lessons in it. Life lessons that I learned along the way. It had things that I didn't want to forget. Moments that changed me, touched me, some for the better and some for the not so better. I guess I'd figure all that out later.

It's strange the things that happen in your life that touch you and you never even know about it. It's like throwing pebbles in water. As the pebbles create ripples, each ripple interacts with another ripple and causes a whole new ripple effect. I guess that's how my life is. What I do affects others as much as it affects me. I picked up my pen and started writing.

"What I do, the choices I make, have consequences. These consequences don't just affect me. I need to learn to make choices that I can live with so that I can live with myself."

I stopped writing and looked up thinking.

I wasted the past few months being mad at life, at everybody and everything. I can't say that I'm not still mad 'cause I know I still am. But I need to find a way to channel my anger. I don't know if it's through dance or books or gardening, but I have to do something better than what I *was* doing. Whatever, changes have to be made, definitely.

I also knew that I had people around me that would help me through this. People I loved, my grandmother, Jade, my girls, my dad, Terrence. I even had people I wasn't too sure about like Li'l T and Dr. Tubbs. The thing was, I needed to step up. I had been going fast in the wrong direction. Now it was time to change all that. I wrote again.

"My grandmother is a trip. I can't believe the things she does sometimes. She's like the pictures on the wall in the living room. On the surface it's just a picture, but beneath there's so much more. What would I do without her?"

I stopped writing. I was thinking that I'd try to hold on to this book for my kids—if I ever do have kids. Jade was right. We'll never be able to place our babies in our mom's arms, but we could make sure that some part of her lives through us. She made mistakes. I made mistakes, and more than likely, I'll make a lot more. But I'll learn something each time. And maybe be a little better for it. I wrote a few more sentences then closed my recipe book.

My cell rang. I answered. "Girl, where the hell were you last night? I looked all over the school grounds. Then I called and left you like a hundred messages. This had better be good," Ursula said angrily.

"What are you talking about? I was looking for you."

"Cassie came over and said that you were in trouble and that you needed me to go to the school and help you. I got there, and it was locked up tight. What happened? Where were you?"

"Cassie called me and told me that you were in trouble. I went over to her house and then to your house. Darien and Cassie were there."

"I know. They were there when I left to find you. They were getting high as usual."

"Yeah, I saw that."

"You didn't go inside, did you?"

"Yeah, I did. Cassie left as soon as I got there."

"Cassie is such a bitch. She'll do anything Darien tells her to do as long as he was gonna give her a bag. You know about the fight, right?"

"Yeah"

"It was because of me."

"What, how so?"

"When I was at your house and after Cassie left, Darien started acting all crazy. He ripped my shirt, and I hit him with some of his stupid trophies."

Ursula broke up laughing. "Oh, yeah, I love it. You know you broke his arm, don't you?"

"Are you kidding me?" I said, surprised.

"Nope, for real, my mom told me that's what the ambulance tech told her."

"Oh, crap, I know he's pissed."

"I wouldn't worry about it. His time's up."

"What do you mean?"

"He's in major trouble. He had a concealed weapon, so his juvie pass is expired."

I know I was probably tired but for real I had no idea what she was talking about. "Huh?"

"The cops caught him with a gun in his pants, plus

everybody told them that he was the one who pulled the knife on TB. Do you believe he actually said that TB pulled the knife on him like before?"

"Like before, what do you mean?" I asked.

"Well, yeah, before TB did go after him with a knife, but that was because of his little brother. He was so pissed at D. Anyway, they both got sent to juvie hall for that. But it's the gun thing that got D this time. Apparently they checked, and it was used in an armed robbery and a shooting."

"You sound almost happy about it," I said, seeing somebody running down the street. The first thing I thought about was more trouble coming. But then the runner kind of looked familiar.

"Let's just say I'm not mad at how it turned out. D is an asshole. He's a bully and a joke. I'm so glad that he's gonna be out of the house again and that ain't about no sibling rivalry. D is dangerous and anybody hooked up with him had better back off. His dad saw it, and now my mom finally sees that. Plus some guy at the go-go said that D stabbed him."

I wasn't surprised. Darien was seriously headed to prison or to an early grave. It was only a matter of time. He went faster and faster with everything he did. He was mad about his life, but instead of doing something to change it, he just got madder and madder and went faster and faster.

"What about Sierra?" I asked, still checking out the runner coming down the street. I saw that it was Terrence.

Ursula laughed again. "That's the tight part. D always had Sierra as his back. She would lie for him and everything. But not this time. She stepped up and nailed his coffin. She told the police everything. D is in so much trouble. Anyway, I gotta go. Oh, girl, I didn't I tell you the best part about D."

"You know what Ursula," I said as I stood up and walked down the brick path to the steps and waited. "I don't want to hear it. I'm putting all this behind me, especially Darien and his drama."

"A'ight, sounds good to me, I might just do the same thing. I'll call you later." Then she hung up.

Terrence stopped running when he got in front of the house. We just looked at each other for a minute. He was breathing hard from his run, so I let him catch his breath. "So," I finally said, "when did you start running at dawn?"

"When I started at Howard. It helps clear my head."

"Maybe I should start, join you," I said half joking.

"Nah, not a good idea," he said, touching the tiny scar still on his face from where I once accidently scratched him when I ran away. "When you run, you get violent. I just saw Li'l T. He's got a black eye." We smiled, knowing exactly what he meant.

"You left me."

"What?" he said, still out of breath.

"You heard me. You went off to college and left me. Everybody did—you, Jade, mom. I was alone for the first time and I was scared."

"That's just it, you were never alone, Kenisha. You had me, Jade, your friends and your grandmother. That's not alone. You just chose the easy way out."

"I know. It was a bad choice," I said. He nodded then

looked down the street. I looked at him. This is lawn mower guy, probably the first guy to actually like me for me and not what he could get from me. He always made me feel special, and he never patronized me. We had our battles at first, but in the end, I knew that I could always count on him. I don't know why I forgot that.

"So what now?" he asked.

"So I think maybe it's time to slow down," I said.

He nodded. "That's perhaps a good idea. It's hard, yes, but you can do it. You have plenty of support."

"Yeah, I know I can." I took a deep breath, "I was accepted back at Hazelhurst starting next semester," I said, bursting to tell someone.

His face brightened. "Congratulations," he said, smiling at me. His dimple winked, and I couldn't help but fall for him all over again. After all, he was my lawn mower guy.

"And," I said, considering telling him this, but decided that he'd understand and support me, "I was thinking of going back to the shrink my dad took me to before." I began stepping down off the top step to street level. We just started walking.

"A shrink?" he said surprised. "What, you crazy now?" he joked.

We looked at each other and laughed. It was an easy moment that felt good for both of us. "Yeah, his name is Tubbs, and he's about eighty-eight years old, but he's cool. A little twisted, but cool."

"He sounds perfect for you."

"Yeah, I think so." Actually I surprised myself when I

said that. But for real, I meant it. Maybe Tubbs was right. It's okay to be mad at my mom, as long as I still love her. Why not? So lawn mower guy and I kept walking, strolling actually, slow and easy, like we had all the time in the world. Neither one of us was in any hurry to get anywhere anytime soon.

QUESTIONS FOR DISCUSSION

1. At the beginning of the story, Kenisha feels emotionally distant from the rest of her classmates. She seems troubled, and her father and friends don't understand why. What circumstances contribute to Kenisha's feeling of isolation? What would you suggest she do to get back to her usual self? Have you ever felt this way?

2. Early on in the book, Kenisha has a fight and is given one last chance to behave herself in order to remain at Hazelhurst Academy. Provoked by Chili, she lashes out. How could she have handled the situation better? Was her expulsion fair, given the warning, even though this fight wasn't her fault? How would you have handled it?

3. There are several people around Kenisha who can help her through this difficult time, but she refuses to talk to them. Why do you think she closes herself off from her friends, family and Terrence?

4. *Fast Forward* takes place at two very different schools—Penn Hall High School and Hazelhurst Academy. How are the two schools different in Kenisha's eyes?

5. Kenisha's school records and problems follow her to Penn Hall. How would you overcome a bad reputation if you were in her situation?

6. Who is the antagonist in *Fast Forward* and how does this person manipulate others? What is this person's motivation?

7. Kenisha pushes away Terrence, Jalisa and Diamond. Why do you think she does that, but allows Darien into her life?

8. Kenisha knows exactly what kind of person Darien is, yet she chooses to hang out with him anyway. It isn't until things get dangerous that she backs off. Why do you think she is so tempted by his "bad boy" personality?

9. Some of the choices Kenisha's made have serious consequences. How can you make sure that the choices you make are good ones?

10. At the beginning of each chapter, Kenisha's MySpace entries offer insight into her life. Are there any entries that you can relate to, and why?

Fifteen-year-old Kenisha Lewis has it all.
Or so she thought.

Pushing Pause

Celeste O. Norfleet

Kenisha Lewis has a good life, filled with hip
friends, a hot boyfriend, loving parents and a
bling-filled home in the burbs. But suddenly
that all changes. She loses her stable family life,
her boyfriend dumps her and her friends are
acting weird. Could things be any worse? Time
for Kenisha to push the pause button on her life
and take a long, deep breath…

*Available the first week of October
wherever books are sold.*